Sienna Mercer

TAIL SPIN

EGMONT

EGMONT

We bring stories to life

With special thanks to Lisa Fiedler

My Brother the Werewolf: Tail Spin first published in Great Britain 2014
by Egmont UK Limited
The Yellow Building, 1 Nicholas Road, London W11 4AN

Copyright © Working Partners Ltd 2014
Created by Working Partners Limited, London WC1X 9HH

ISBN 978 1 4052 6798 4

1 3 5 7 9 10 8 6 4 2

A CIP catalogue record for this title is available from the British
Library

Typeset by Avon DataSet Ltd, Bidford on Avon, Warwickshire
Printed and bound in Great Britain by the CPI Group

55612/1

Please note: Any website addresses listed in this book are correct at the time of going to print.
However, Egmont cannot take responsibility for any third party content or advertising. Please
be aware that online content can be subject to change and websites can contain content that is
unsuitable for children. We advise that all children are supervised when using the internet.

EGMONT LUCKY COIN

Our story began over a century ago, when seventeen-year-old
Egmont Harald Petersen found a coin in the street.

He was on his way to buy a flyswatter, a small hand-operated
printing machine that he then set up in his tiny apartment.

The coin brought him such good luck that today Egmont has
offices in over 30 countries around the world. And that lucky
coin is still kept at the company's head offices in Denmark.

To Shannon, who rocks

Chapter One

Daniel Packer wasn't scared. He was just . . . what was that new word he was trying to learn for the vocabulary test?

'C'mon, cub,' said his twin brother, Justin, who was standing beside him. 'You can do this.'

Daniel recognised the tone. It was Justin's 'game voice' – the one he used before football matches when he wanted to psych himself up.

But Daniel's feet seemed stuck to the driveway.

'What's the problem?' Justin demanded.

'I'm just feeling a little *trepidatious*,' Daniel

muttered, finally finding the word he was looking for.

Justin thumped his brother on the back. 'Fear is for the weak, cubby!'

Please! What did Justin know about fear? It was one thing to be brave when all you had to do was sprint across a football field through a maze of huge, hulking opponents. *Ringing your dream-girl's doorbell and making conversation with her parents requires a whole different level of guts*, Daniel thought.

'Hey, Daniel,' came Riley's voice from the other side of Justin. 'If you're worried about Debi's dad liking you, just think how much better your chances of impressing him will be if you show up *on time*.' She checked her watch and sighed. 'Besides, those of us who have to rely on regular coats instead of werewolf fur would *really* appreciate being indoors.'

Daniel frowned. 'In case you hadn't noticed,

Riley, I'm not in wolf-form at the moment.' This was actually a miracle. In the past, a panic of this magnitude would have had Daniel's inner wolf revealing itself in a big way. That's why he'd worn a long, hooded jacket that covered most of his body – he always had to allow for sudden fur-sproutage.

Riley reached out and pressed the doorbell. After a moment, the door opened slightly and Debi wriggled out through the narrow space. 'Hi, guys,' she said.

Daniel gulped. She looked amazing. Her brilliant red hair was pulled up loosely into a bun and lots of wispy curls bobbed around her face. She was wearing a pretty navy blue dress with a flouncy skirt; her red pea-coat was draped over her arm. Debi's eyes sparkled when Justin and Riley cried out, 'Happy Birthday!'

Half-mesmerised by how awesome she

looked, Daniel's own 'Happy Birthday' came out a second or two behind theirs.

Fortunately, Debi didn't seem to notice. 'Thanks,' she said. 'I'm so glad you guys could make it.'

'So are we,' said Riley, nodding towards the door. 'But, um, is there any way we could come inside and warm up a little?'

'Actually . . .' Debi's dazzling smile faltered as she quickly shrugged her coat on. 'My parents won't be long, we can wait out here.'

'No problem,' Daniel agreed, relieved about holding off the parental encounter for a while longer. But Mr Morgan's voice boomed from the other side of the door.

'Debi! I need a few more minutes, sweetie,' said Mr Morgan. 'You'd better bring your friends inside.'

Daniel's super-hearing picked up Riley's, '*Thank*

goodness,' whispered through chattering teeth.

'But, Dad,' Debi called back, 'we have a seven o'clock reservation.'

'I won't be long,' her father promised.

Daniel could just see him in the hall behind Debi, tapping away at his cellphone's screen. 'I'm just going to finish this call in private.' He stopped to give his daughter a pointed look. 'You and your friends can wait in the living room.'

When Debi mumbled a reply, Daniel's turbocharged hearing picked it up loud and clear:

'*Like I'd let them wait anywhere else.*'

What did *that* mean?

Debi bit her lip. 'OK,' she said at last. 'Come on in, guys.'

As Debi pushed open the door, Daniel realised that he'd never actually been inside her house before. He followed his brother into the Morgans' hall . . .

. . . and found himself standing in the dark.

'Did a bulb blow out?' he asked, blinking into the shadows.

'No,' said Debi, stepping away from the light switch hurriedly. 'Just thought it might be nice to . . . be in the dark.'

Her statement was followed by a loud crash.

I could have guessed Riley would find a way to walk into a coat rack, Daniel thought.

He shuffled across the darkened hall and reached out blindly to pat his girlfriend's shoulder. 'Is everything OK?' he asked.

'Everything's fine,' Debi answered.

Unfortunately, her voice came from the opposite side of the hall.

'Debi, why are the lights out?' The voice in the dark was deep . . . and coming from just above the place where Daniel's hand was resting!

In the next second, the lights flicked on and

Daniel found himself with his hand planted on Justin's shoulder. He pulled it away fast.

I thought Debi seemed a little tall!

'This way, guys,' Debi said.

Before they exited the hall, Daniel's wolf ears caught a snippet of Mr Morgan's phone conversation from the bedroom.

'I know Serena didn't turn up anything conclusive,' Mr Morgan was saying, 'but I suspect she was closer to the truth than even *she* realised.'

He tuned the voice out and followed Debi. Being shuffled off to the living room was a good thing. It would give him the chance to present Debi with her gift away from her parents' scrutinising eyes.

Excellent.

He was pretty sure she would like it, because Riley had gushed over the necklace, assuring him that Debi would *absolutely love* it. But still, maybe

Riley had misjudged. Maybe Debi hated shells. Maybe she hated necklaces. Maybe she hated birthday presents in general! Maybe it wasn't so excellent . . .

All these worries about her not liking it had left the palms of Daniel's hands seriously sweaty.

How can I hand Debi her present with slimy hands?!

'Mind if I use your bathroom?' he asked quickly.

Again, Debi looked worried. She shot a glance down the hall and sighed. 'Go to the end of the hallway and take a right. It's the second door on the left.'

'Got it,' said Daniel, as Debi and the others continued towards the living room.

But at the end of the hall, he hesitated, realising he'd been so worried about her seeing his hands, he hadn't really listened to what she had said. Was he supposed to turn left or right?

He tossed a coin in his head, turned left and opened the second door on the right . . .

Daniel stared into the room, eyes wide. *Wrong!* This was definitely *not* the bathroom!

Wait . . . What in the world is this place . . . ?

It was weird enough that the entire room was wallpapered with curled, yellowed newspaper clippings and huge antique maps with red pins stuck in them. But what was up with that *smell*?

It wasn't that it was unfamiliar, it was just the fact that it seemed to be magnified a zillion times that made it difficult to identify. Daniel's nose twitched as he tried to name the aroma, but for some reason, all he could think about was giant pizzas.

Unable to fight his curiosity, he stepped into the room for a better look. Many of the old maps were of far-off places that Daniel had only heard of: Hungary, Bulgaria, Romania . . .

9

Two were of Debi's hometown. One appeared to be several hundred years old. The name of the town was written across the top edge in elaborate, old-fashioned letters.

Franklin Grove

The ancient map was labelled to show the location of the Blacksmith's Shoppe, the Hallowed Burial Ground, the Healer's Cottage and the Office of the Constable.

The second map, posted below the old one, was much newer. It included the locations of Sudsy's Car Wash, a Mister Smoothie, Franklin Grove Middle School and, oddly, a retail space marked Future Site of the FoodMart.

Scattered on a table beneath these large maps were a handful of smaller ones – street maps. These maps were also from Franklin Grove, and every single one was marked with several large question marks, drawn in purple marker.

Daniel's nose still twitched at the powerful smell in the room, but he barely noticed. He walked to the bookcase on the far wall, which was crammed with dusty old tomes. In one corner stood a suit of armour: poised with one arm lifted high above the helmet, its metal gauntlet clutching a deadly-looking battle axe! Next to the armour, on a battered wooden filing cabinet, stood a scarred wooden cross. On a table next to that was a silver flask with a sticky label that read, 'Holy Water'.

'There you are,' came Debi's voice.

Daniel spun around to see Debi in the doorway. She was trying to smile but couldn't quite dredge one up. She looked totally embarrassed.

'Hey,' said Justin, striding into the room. 'It smells delicious in here.'

Debi winced and Daniel followed her eye line. In the corner, a long braided rope of giant garlic bulbs hung on a nail. Daniel had been too entranced with the maps to notice it before. Now he realised that there were large baskets of the stuff placed all around the room.

So *that* was the familiar pizza-like aroma! Garlic. Lots of perfectly normal people kept garlic in their houses – but they probably stored it in the kitchen. And Daniel was pretty sure they didn't collect lifetime supplies of it.

'Cool room,' said Riley, coming in behind Justin and admiring the suit of armour. 'I'm totally into antiques.' Then suddenly she held her nose. 'But what's with all the garlic?'

Debi let out a long sigh. 'It's nothing,' she said. 'My dad just has a bit of a hobby.'

Daniel gazed around the room again, wondering what connected garlic, wooden crosses and holy water . . .

Then he realised. 'Oh,' he said, looking straight at Debi, whose gaze fell to the floor.

'Yeah,' she said, her shoulders up by her chin. 'My dad kind of . . . sort of . . . believes – or, *thinks* – that there could be real-live vampires living in our old hometown.'

She tried to roll her eyes, but didn't quite pull it off.

Daniel could tell she was mortified by this strange family secret. 'Maybe your dad had good reason to believe it,' he suggested cautiously. 'I mean, there are plenty of things in the world that people can't explain.'

'I guess,' Debi allowed. 'But, *vampires*?'

'Vampires suck,' said Justin, then laughed at his own joke. Daniel gave his twin a look, and he immediately fell silent.

'Sorry,' he said. 'I couldn't resist.'

'It's fine,' said Debi. 'It's so outrageous, you kind of have to laugh. We had a large goth population at school – in fact, almost half the people in town stayed as pale as paper, even in summer – but, *still* . . . All that proves is that sunscreen really works. Right?'

No one said a word. Debi cocked an eyebrow. 'Why isn't this freaking you guys out?' she asked.

Because we're not exactly unfamiliar with the concept of supernatural townsfolk, Daniel thought grimly.

Riley was the first to realise that their lack of surprise might seem strange.

'Oh, it *is* freaking us out,' she quickly assured Debi. 'I just always feel extra safe when I have Justin close by.' She turned a glowing smile towards Justin, who beamed back at her.

'I'm glad to hear that,' Debi said. 'Because since we moved to Pine Wood, my dad's been working on another theory.'

'What's that?' Daniel asked, in as casual a tone as he could manage, but he was terrified to hear the answer. 'Covens of witches? Bigfoot? Aliens?' He attempted to laugh, but it came out sounding more like a nervous croak.

'You're not far off,' Debi sighed. 'He thinks there's something spooky going on up around Lycan Point.'

Daniel instantly stuffed his hands into his pockets, just in case there was a fur explosion. He *knew* there was something going on up around Lycan Point. He was one of the spooky things!

'This is going to sound even weirder than the vampires,' said Debi, 'but Dad thinks Pine Wood might be home to a pack of . . .' she blushed as she said, 'werewolves.'

Daniel kept his mouth clamped shut, certain that anything he attempted to say would come out not as words, but a long and blood-curdling howl.

They found Mr and Mrs Morgan standing in the driveway next to their SUV.

'I'm so glad you kids could join us,' Mrs Morgan said, smiling around at the group. 'I'm sure you're all going to love the double chocolate raspberry cake.'

'I'm sure we will,' said Justin, giving her a big grin, then reaching out to shake Mr Morgan's hand. 'Thank you both for inviting us.'

Daniel noticed Riley looking impressed by her boyfriend's manners, and wished he could impress Debi by showing the same kind of manners. But offering his host a hairy paw might raise difficult questions. Mr Morgan let go of

Justin's hand, then swung around to offer Daniel a handshake. Thinking fast, Daniel tugged his paw far up into his sleeve then held out his arm in Mr Morgan's direction, like a wave.

'Got something against shaking hands, son?' Mr Morgan asked.

'No, sir. It's just . . . uh . . .'

'It's a rock-star thing,' Justin said. 'Daniel's gotta keep his hands safe if he wants to strum that guitar.'

The grunt of annoyance from Mr Morgan made Daniel even more nervous – he could feel spiny whiskers beginning to push through the skin around his nose.

'What about that hood?' Mr Morgan asked. 'Do rock stars have to hide their faces, too?'

'The paparazzi are chasing him,' Justin said.

This got everyone laughing, even Debi's dad. Daniel tried to join in but when his laugh came

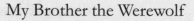

out sounding like a wolfish whine, he clamped his mouth shut.

'Let's get going,' said Debi. 'I've been waiting all year for this birthday dinner.'

She opened the car door, and a burst of hot, dry air escaped.

Mrs Morgan sighed and slipped off her coat. 'The heat's up too high. Kids, you might want to take your jackets off for the ride.'

Debi, Riley and Justin obediently removed their coats. Daniel, of course, just stood there.

As Debi slid into the middle section of the SUV, Justin and Riley climbed into the third row in back.

Mr Morgan stood in the driveway, frowning at Daniel.

'It's about 82 degrees in that vehicle,' Mr Morgan pointed out, tossing his own jacket into the car. 'You might want to shed that oversized sleeping bag you're wearing.'

Please don't say 'shed', Daniel thought, trying not to imagine leaving clumps of fuzzy wolf fur all over the back seat of the Morgan's car.

'I'm still a little chilly,' he lied, letting his fangs chatter. 'I'll just leave it on until we get to Chez . . .' and now he'd forgotten the name of Debi's favourite restaurant! '. . . Thingy.'

The look on Mr Morgan's face said it was the opposite of 'OK'. But there was nothing Daniel could do except duck into the overheated car beside Debi. The puffed-up nylon fabric of his jacket made a swishy, whistling sound as he buckled up.

Humiliating!

As Mr Morgan backed the SUV out of the driveway, Daniel willed himself to calm down. He had to be completely de-wolfed by the time they arrived at Chez Thingy so he would be able to leave his giant jacket in the coatroom like everybody else.

In the front seat, Mrs Morgan sniffed the hot air and frowned. 'This is going to sound odd, but does anyone else smell . . . burning *fur*?'

Daniel sunk into his seat and bit back a howl of misery.

This was going to be a long ride.

Chapter Two

From the minute they stepped inside the restaurant, Justin felt as though he were trespassing. Chez Claude was without a doubt Pine Wood's classiest dining establishment. Its gigantic crystal chandeliers, gleaming china place settings, fresh flowers in elegant vases and tall candles flickering in what were probably solid gold candlesticks made it look like a royal palace.

After they'd all left their coats in the cloakroom – except for Daniel – they followed the head waiter to their table. Justin noticed that people were staring at his brother. Every time

Daniel's puffy nylon sleeves brushed against his sides of the jacket, they made a *sweeszh-sweeszh-sweeszh* sound.

'What's with the death-grip?' Justin whispered to Riley. She had been holding his hand since the moment they'd handed over their coats, grasping his fingers so tightly, he was afraid that when they finally got their meals he wouldn't be able to hold his knife and fork.

'I don't want to fall over in such an elegant place,' Riley whispered back.

'Don't worry,' Justin told her. 'I'll catch you.'

They took their seats around the table. Justin sat on Riley's left, the best position to keep her from trashing the place.

The head waiter was giving Daniel a cold look. His French accent sounded not-very-impressed: 'Perhaps *Monsieur* would care to remove his jacket?'

Daniel seemed to take the hint and unzipped the parka. Thankfully, he looked fur-free!

While a tuxedoed busboy filled their crystal water goblets, Mr Morgan asked a waiter to bring snails for the whole table. OK, he actually said 'escargot', but still – they could give it whatever fancy name they liked, it did *not* make Justin any more eager to eat it.

'What about if we all give the birthday girl her gifts now?' said Mrs Morgan.

Debi's eyes lit up. 'Really?'

'I know my girl,' said Mrs Morgan, patting Debi's hand. 'If we don't do it now, she'll be so distracted wondering what she's getting, she won't be able to enjoy her meal.'

Debi put her head in her hands. 'Way to make me look spoiled, Mom,' she groaned.

'We'll go first,' said Riley, reaching down to retrieve her purse from beneath the table. As she did, her shoulder bumped the edge, making her water glass wobble. Justin stretched across her bread plate and caught it before even a drop could spill.

'Here you go,' Riley said, handing over a beautifully wrapped gift. 'This is from Justin and me.'

Debi's eyes danced with excitement as she pulled off the paper, letting the shredded remains fall where they may. 'It's a Count Vira book!' Debi cried with delight, holding up the hardcover and showing an image of a moon shining on a still lake, with a brooding vampire staring at his – too handsome – reflection. The title of the book was *Everlasting Night*.

'Who's Count Vira?' Daniel asked.

Both girls gawked at him.

'Only the greatest writer ever,' said Debi. 'I have the whole series – except this one. It just came out a week ago.' She leaned over to hug Riley. 'Thank you. I love it.'

'Let me have a look,' said Mr Morgan.

'No way,' giggled Debi, flipping through the crisp new pages. 'You're not getting your hands on it until I've finished.'

Riley looked amazed. 'Mr Morgan, *you* like Count Vira?'

Not surprising, thought Justin. *The guy's obsessed with vampires.*

'It's a guilty pleasure,' Mr Morgan confessed. 'Have you heard they're making a movie out of *Eternal Sunset?*'

'Of course,' said Riley.

'And,' said Debi, grinning widely, '*Jackson Caulfield* is playing the romantic lead.'

For a minute, Justin was afraid Riley might actually faint. She tried to speak but seemed unable to get any words out.

'You mean romantic *leads* . . . plural,' Mr Morgan corrected. 'The parts of the identical twin brothers who fall for the vampire sisters Belinda and Carmina are both going to be played by Jefferson Caulfield.'

'*Jackson* Caulfield!' Debi and Riley cried in unison.

Debi passed her new book around the table. When Daniel fanned through the pages, Justin noticed something written on the inside of the front cover.

'It's got writing in it,' he whispered to Riley. 'Did we have it signed by the author or something?'

His answer was a firm elbow to the ribs. 'No!' she whispered back. 'I inscribed it. That's what you do when you give someone a book.' Riley took the book from Daniel and showed it to Justin. 'See? I even signed your name for you.'

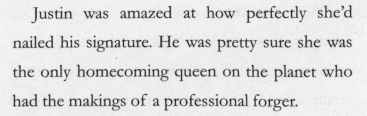

Justin was amazed at how perfectly she'd nailed his signature. He was pretty sure she was the only homecoming queen on the planet who had the makings of a professional forger.

'It would have been cool if we could have had Count Viral sign it for you,' he said, handing the book back to Debi.

'You mean Count *Vira*,' said Debi. 'And yes, that would have been awesome, but virtually impossible. The books are actually written by a woman named Winifred Peters, and she's a total recluse. Count Vira is her pen name.'

'She never does book signings,' Riley sighed. 'If she ever did, I would *so* go.'

'Me too,' said Debi.

Mrs Morgan leaned forwards to interrupt. 'Moving on with the birthday gifts . . .' she said, producing an elegantly wrapped box and placing it in front of Debi. 'This one is from Dad and me.'

27

The minute Debi took the present from her mother, Justin noticed that his brother's nose began to twitch. His eyes were watering.

'What's up?' Justin asked in the softest whisper he could manage. He knew only Daniel would hear him.

Daniel replied with a shrug. He was practically trembling now, pressing his lips together as his nose wiggled and twitched like a crazed rabbit's.

Luckily, Debi wasn't noticing his weird behaviour. Her eyes were dancing over the pretty paper and ribbon. 'I guess it's not a pony,' she teased her parents.

Debi tore into the paper and gasped when she saw the name 'Jewellery on Main' written in golden script across the top. Opening the box, she removed a delicate silver chain with charms hanging from it.

'I love it!' she breathed.

Justin watched his brother's already contorted face go straight to 'devastated'.

Silver! A werewolf's kryptonite!

Daniel began to sniffle the minute Debi slipped the bracelet on to her left wrist and dangled it in front of his face.

'Isn't it gorgeous?' she asked. 'I'll never take it off!'

A girlfriend in possession of a silver bracelet would be the challenge of a lifetime for Daniel! Lupine blood never reacted well when silver was near. It wasn't deadly; it just gave a werewolf the uncontrollable urge to . . .

'*Ah . . . Ah . . . Ahhhhhhhh –*'

Justin watched in horror as Daniel's whole face crinkled up into something out of a special-effects-heavy alien movie. For one crazy second, Justin considered ducking under the table.

'*– Choooooooooooooo!*'

29

The explosion of sound caused Riley to jump right off her seat. She crashed into a passing waiter, who was balancing a tray of beverages above his head.

The waiter wobbled; the tray bobbled . . .

As Justin gaped, everything seemed to happen in slow motion. The tray tipped dangerously as the waiter struggled to regain his balance. For one second it looked as though he might have it under control, but then he lost his grip. Five of the six glasses crashed to the floor . . . but one – a goblet of cranberry juice – sailed towards Riley.

Justin reacted as he would have on the football field with one of Kyle Hunter's bullet passes zooming towards him – he leapt off his chair, pushing Riley's head down towards the table with one hand while reaching for the cranberry-and-glass missile with the other, catching it as neatly as if it were a football.

The good news was, Justin had kept Riley dry. The bad news was, he couldn't stop the juice spraying out of the glass like a geyser, into his face and hair, turning him into a dripping, sticky, cranberry-scented mess.

The entire restaurant went silent as everyone turned to stare.

It was in this moment of silence that the waiter arrived with their escargots . . . six individual appetiser plates, each with its own tiny sterling *silver* fork!

Daniel managed to sniffle out a heartfelt apology before covering his face in his hands and launching into a sneezing frenzy.

Mr Morgan sat back in his chair, folding his arms and muttering: 'This is not how I pictured this dinner going.'

'It isn't Daniel's fault,' said Riley, sounding like she was holding back tears. 'He can't help having a cold. The mess is my fault . . . because I'm the world's biggest klutz.'

With that, she stood up from her chair, which fell over with a clatter as she dashed out of the dining area.

Justin stood there clutching the empty glass as cranberry juice dribbled down his face.

He saw Debi staring at him. 'What are you waiting for?' she asked.

Justin put the glass down, hopped over the upturned chair, and ran after Riley.

He found her pacing the fancy lobby.

'Are you OK?' he asked.

'Of course I'm OK,' she huffed. '*I'm* always OK. It's the people *around* me who wind up bruised or battered, or . . .' she motioned to his wet hair and drippy face '. . . totally soaked with juice. Anybody who comes within ten feet of me puts their life on the line.'

'At most, it was my hairdo on the line,' Justin joked.

'Stop pretending you don't mind.'

'But I *don't* mind,' Justin assured her. 'You're totally worth it. Besides, it brings an awful lot of adventure into my life.'

That got a smile out of her. 'Speaking of adventure . . . I'm thinking about trying something that'll help me solve my klutziness conundrum.'

'What is it?' asked Justin, unable to imagine what sort of adventure could de-klutz-ify a person.

Riley beamed. 'Dance class.' She waved in a jazz hands fashion.

'Dance class?' That didn't sound especially adventurous, but then again, for Riley, tying on a pair of ballet slippers could present as much of a hazard as zip-lining across the Grand Canyon. He shrugged. 'Go for it.'

'Not *me*,' she said, stepping closer. '*We*.'

Oh . . . Justin felt the blood drain from his face.

'*We?*' he repeated. 'As in you and me . . . *dancing?*'

This just went from 'adventure' to 'foolish escapade'.

Helping your girlfriend avoid injury on a daily basis was one thing. Attending dance class with her – and risking the Beasts on the football team finding out about it – was something else.

Still . . . this was *Riley.*

He grinned. 'Like I said,' he whispered, 'you're worth it. Now let's get back in there.'

As they made their way back to the dining area, Riley wrapped her arms around him and squeezed. Justin allowed himself to enjoy the hug and relish the knowledge that his girlfriend was thrilled with him.

Because, when the Beasts got wind of this dancing thing, he was pretty sure *they* would be anything but 'thrilled'.

Daniel didn't care that it was freezing outside — he needed to get out of this restaurant fast. With his giant jacket flapping behind him, he grabbed his brother's arm and jerked him out the door.

'You could have waited for me to get my gloves on,' Justin grumbled. 'It's like the Arctic out here.'

'I couldn't take it any more,' Daniel said. 'That place was crawling with silver.'

'Yeah,' said Justin. 'I thought Mr Morgan was gonna have a heart attack when you started eating with your fingers.'

Daniel groaned. Sloppy as it was, he'd had no choice but to eat his snails with his hands. And as if that weren't pathetic enough, he hadn't even given Debi her gift.

'Explain to me,' said Justin now, as if he were

reading Daniel's mind, 'why you pretended you forgot Debi's present.'

Daniel shook his head. 'It couldn't have compared to the Silver Doom.'

Justin began to chuckle at the nickname Daniel had come up with for Debi's new bracelet, but immediately caught himself. 'What do you mean?'

'That bracelet came from some glitzy jewellery store and cost a zillion bucks,' Daniel explained. 'The necklace *I* bought her is made out of seashells . . . which you can find on the beach for free.'

Justin nodded. 'But Debi's not hung up on how much stuff costs. I'm pretty sure she'd love it just because it's from you.'

'Maybe. But Mr Morgan's a different story. What if he'd seen that necklace and decided that I was the stingiest cheapskate in Pine Wood?'

Justin sighed. 'I think you should have just given her the necklace.'

'I know.' Daniel kicked at a pebble on the sidewalk. 'But *my* gift is the least of my problems. It's her parents' gift that's going to make my life miserable.'

'Yeah,' Justin agreed. 'If she never takes that off, you're going to go into a sneezing fit every time you try to hold her hand. And take it from someone who knows about hand-holding – there's going to be a lot of those times.'

'There's more to worry about than that,' said Daniel. 'If Mr Morgan is already suspicious about werewolves, I'm sure he's studied the folklore. What if he puts it together . . . the silver bracelet, my sneezing fit . . .?'

Suddenly, Daniel stopped talking; he'd caught a whiff of an odd scent that *definitely* wasn't garlic.

'Are you gonna sneeze again?' Justin asked,

taking a step backwards.

Daniel didn't answer. The smell was getting stronger and he knew exactly what it was: *wolf!*

Pine Wood was full of Lupines, even though human form was the mode in which they spent 99.999 per cent of their time – but Daniel had caught the scent of a fully transformed werewolf!

'What's up?' asked Justin.

Daniel quickly explained that he was pretty sure there was a werewolf in the immediate area. He followed his nose along the row of manicured shrubbery. At the end of the hedges, he dropped to his hands and knees in the flowerbeds.

There in the soil was a large, slender paw print.

'I knew it!' Daniel cried, just as Justin began calling out, as if Daniel was all the way down the street:

'Bro, how's the search going? Did you find your *contact lens* yet?'

'What are you –' Turning, Daniel stopped himself before he said too much.

Debi, Riley and the Morgans stood a few feet behind Justin, staring in disbelief.

'Daniel sneezed,' Justin explained.

'What a shock,' said Mr Morgan.

'Right,' said Daniel, scampering to his feet and brushing the dirt from his hands. 'I sneezed . . . and one of my contact lenses fell right out of my eye!'

Debi eyed him strangely. 'I didn't know you wore contact lenses.'

'Well, uh . . . I don't, usually. I was just trying these out. I thought tinted contact lenses might give me a funky look when I'm playing my guitar on stage.'

'But your eyes didn't look different tonight,' Debi observed.

'They didn't?' Daniel shrugged. 'Waste of

money!' He pretended to remove the remaining contact lens and flick it into the bushes.

Mr Morgan was looking at Daniel with a strange expression. Not just irritated, but . . . suspicious.

The parking attendant arrived with the SUV and everyone climbed in. Since Debi was wearing her new bracelet on her left wrist, Daniel made sure to sit on her right. He managed to limit himself to three sneezes during the ride home.

But it was still a miserable trip. He couldn't stop himself from wondering:

Will I be able to make this up to Debi?

And, why is a Lupine roaming the town in full wolf form?

Chapter Three

Daniel felt like a coward, hiding behind his locker door, but he didn't have a choice – Debi was on the other side, wielding Silver Doom like a sparkly weapon. Since the metal door acted as a barrier to the nasty effects of the bracelet, he was taking his time arranging his books in the locker.

'I can't believe I forgot your present again,' he said, speaking into the locker. It gave his words a tinny echo, making his lie sound even worse to his guilty ears. 'I guess I left it on my dresser this morning. But it'll be worth the wait. I promise.'

Debbie giggled. 'You don't have to keep saying that. I have complete faith in your gift-giving abilities!'

Daniel took another gulp of stale locker-air. He was down to his last textbook – in just a few seconds he would have to close the locker door and resume sneezing.

'Um . . . aren't you supposed to be at cheer practice right now?' he asked.

'Technically, yes,' Debi answered. 'But there's a new girl starting school tomorrow and the principal asked me to give her a tour of the campus this afternoon.'

'That's got to be tough, starting school so late in the semester,' Daniel observed.

Now Debi glanced up at the wall clock and frowned. 'She really should be here by now. The principal said she'd be dropping by at three.'

Dropping . . . Brilliant!

Daniel 'accidentally' jostled the pile of books he'd just arranged, sending them all *dropping* on to the floor.

Debi jumped back to avoid getting her toes smashed by his history textbook.

'Oops,' he said, crouching down to begin the very slow process of picking them up again – safe behind the shield of the open locker door.

'Want some help?' Debi offered.

'*No!* Uh . . . I mean . . . you need to be on the lookout for the new girl. I'm sure she'll be here any minute.' When Daniel reached for his English notebook, he found himself staring at a shiny black shoe firmly planted on one of his books.

Slowly, he looked up. The girl was tall – maybe even taller than Riley, and that was saying something. Her fashion sense was kind of rock 'n' roll, with a hint of goth. But the most striking thing was her hair – it was a toasty-brown colour, but with lots of lighter-toned streaks running through it.

'Hi,' said the girl, bending down to remove the book from beneath her boot. When she saw the title, her glossed lips kicked up at the corners. '*Eternal Sunset*?' she read aloud.

Daniel felt his cheeks grow hot. He'd checked the book out of the school library earlier that morning, planning to read it so that he and Debi would have something else to talk about.

'*Eternal Sunset*?' he said, leaping up from the floor to snatch the book. 'How'd that get there? The librarian must have given me the wrong book – I asked for *Nocturnal Swamp Pet*!'

'You must be Emma Sharpe.' Debi offered the girl a dazzling smile. 'I'm Debi Morgan, your tour guide. And this is my boyfriend, Daniel.'

'Nice to meet you,' said Emma. 'Sorry the

principal's making you do this.'

'It's no trouble at all,' said Debi in her friendly way. 'It'll give us a chance to get to know each other, *and* I can point out which water fountains always spray water in your face.'

Emma laughed. 'Thanks, but I'll stay safe and bring my own.' With that, she took out a blue plastic bottle and helped herself to a long sip.

'You're really going to like it here,' Debi promised. 'It's a great school and everyone's really nice.' She turned a big smile to Daniel and placed her left hand on his arm. 'Isn't that right, Daniel?'

Daniel opened his mouth to say 'yes', but all that came out was an enormous sneeze. *Thank you, Silver Doom*, he thought, pulling a tissue out of his pocket.

'Wow,' said Emma. 'That's some cold you've got there.'

'Yeah,' Daniel muttered.

'And it's not just the school that's so terrific,' Debi continued. 'The town is cool too. In fact, there's a great town-wide event coming up, a fundraiser for the children's hospital. There's going to be all kinds of games and contests – and special guest appearances.'

'Oh, yeah,' said Daniel through his stuffy nose. He'd heard his parents saying something about a fundraiser, but with all the pressure leading up to his girlfriend's birthday dinner, he hadn't thought much about it.

'Why don't you help me show Emma around?' Debi suggested.

'OK,' said Daniel. *As long as I can keep my distance from Silver Doom.*

But before he could make his way to her safe right side, Emma scooted over and beat him to it.

'Great,' muttered Daniel.

'Did you say something?' asked Emma.

'Just . . . *Great!* Let's go!' He tried to sound enthusiastic, but he could tell he was going to be sneezing his way round the cafeteria, the art studio and the library. After a quick trip to the science lab, they made their way outside so Debi could conclude the grand tour at the football field.

'You've got to see our team in action,' Debi told Emma, who wrinkled her nose.

'I'm not much of a football fan,' she admitted.

'Well, you might just become one,' Debi teased, 'after you see The Beasts play.'

Emma shot her a sideways look. 'Did you say *Beasts*?'

Debi nodded. 'Mm-hm. It's kind of a nickname we have for our Offensive squad, because they're so . . . well . . . *wild.*'

'Hmm,' said Emma. 'I guess boys will be boys, right?'

And sometimes they'll be werewolves, Daniel added silently, dabbing his swollen nose with a wad of tissue. He was doing his best to keep some room between himself and the Silver Doom, but with Debi turning back and forth as she described things, it wasn't easy to do.

Now that they were outside, Daniel was happy for the fresh air. As they took a spot along the sidelines he relaxed a bit, his eyes seeking out his brother on the field.

'So how come *you* don't play football?' Emma asked, giving Daniel a long, appraising look. 'You seem like you'd be a natural.'

Woah. Is she . . . flirting *with me?* Daniel automatically took one step closer to Debi.

'*Ooommpf!*'

The sound had come from the fifty yard line, a deep, powerful grunt that (thankfully) called their attention back to the field.

Only now did Daniel realise that the action had stopped. One of the human Defense players, Dylan Porter, had hit the ground hard.

All of the players had come to a stop. The humans (including a very puzzled-looking Justin) were taking advantage of the lull in practice to catch their breath.

The quarterback, Kyle Hunter, and the rest of the Beasts were now staring right at Emma.

That wasn't all that surprising. A new girl in Pine Wood was always a big event. Especially a pretty one, like Emma was.

'Yo!' Kyle bellowed. He was talking to his team, but his eyes were still on Emma. 'Time to quit playing around – I say we run a couple of our more . . . *spectacular* plays! I call, Wild Pack!'

The Beasts cheered, but a groan went up from the Defensive squad, which made Daniel wonder exactly *how* difficult this drill might be.

As the players got into position on the field, Daniel saw Justin approach the quarterback.

'You sure about this, Kyle?' Justin asked. He was mumbling, but Daniel's wolf-ears heard him loud and clear. 'The Wild Pack is a pretty . . . *intense* play.'

'The intense-r the better-er, dude,' Kyle answered. 'I just feel like goin' full speed ahead, ya know?' He bounced on the balls of his feet, as pumped up as if it were a real game.

Which, in a way, it is.

Daniel's thoughts were interrupted by a familiar voice.

'Debi Morgan, where are your pom-poms!?'

Mackenzie Barton, the head cheerleader, was marching towards them with a scowl on her face. This was never a good thing.

'In my locker,' Debi replied calmly. 'When Principal Caine *personally requested* that I give

Emma a tour of the school, I didn't think I'd need to tote my pom-poms along.'

Daniel could actually see Mackenzie deflate. Even the meanest of mean girls recognised that a personal request from the principal totally trumped cheer practice.

'Emma?' Mackenzie snapped. 'Who's Emma?'

'That'd be me,' Emma informed her smoothly. 'I'm new here.'

'Where are you from?' Mackenzie asked with a cool glance at Debi. 'Please don't say Franklin Grove, because I am so *over* that.'

Before Emma could answer, there was another commotion on the football field as the players got into formation. Then Kyle's voice boomed:

'Wild Pack on two! Hut, hut, hike!'

Daniel watched in amazement as the Beasts let loose. The Offense was a blur of motion as players sprinted around the field. The Defense was hopeless against their speed and agility. Even Justin – the only non-Lupine on the Offensive squad – was putting on an impressive show of speed. But it was Caleb Devlin, one of the wide receivers, who stole the show by catching Kyle's sonic-boom of a pass, then evading his blocker with a flawless one-handed front flip, before landing gracefully on his feet to continue his hustle towards the end zone for the touchdown.

They're playing like they're at Lycan Point at night, all alone, Daniel thought, *not at school, during the day – with lots of people around!*

Caleb celebrated his TD with not one, not two, but *three* backflips . . . Then he came to a stop and looked back towards the sidelines, his eyes wide and expectant . . .

. . . and staring right at Emma.

'Looks like someone's trying to impress the new girl,' Mackenzie hissed.

'Actually,' Debi pointed out, 'it looks like *everyone's* trying to impress the new girl.'

Not everyone, thought Daniel, *just the ones with Lupine blood. What's got into these guys? They know there's a new girl at school — someone who has not known them long enough to just accept that* certain *boys at Pine Wood Junior High are just very fast and very strong. They should not strut their werewolf-stuff in broad daylight like this.*

And speaking of strutting . . . Kyle was now strutting across the field to where Daniel and the girls were standing. The quarterback's eyes were focused on Emma, and Daniel couldn't shake the feeling that Kyle looked like a puppy who'd just learned a new trick.

A ferocious supernatural puppy, but still . . .

Just before Kyle reached them, he jumped in the air and executed a perfect back somersault.

'What did you think?' he asked Emma. 'That

was some impressive football, right?'

'Are you asking *me*?' said Emma, her voice level.

'That was an incredible play, Kyle,' Mackenzie piped up in a bubbly voice.

It was like Kyle hadn't heard her. 'We have some mad skills, huh?' he asked Emma.

Mackenzie let out a little squeal of fury as she turned to flounce back to her squad.

'Hunter,' Caleb was calling from the end zone. 'Ask her if she liked my backflips!'

Daniel wondered what had come over these guys. They were always show-offs, but this was on another level.

Emma gave Kyle a cool smile. 'Well, I don't care much for football, but all that flipping and tumbling reminded me of some of the athletes at my old school.'

Kyle glowered. 'No way your football players could do what we just did!'

'Oh, I wasn't talking about our *football* team.' Emma batted her eyes innocently. 'I meant the girls' gymnastics team.'

Daniel felt Debi take a nervous step backwards. He didn't blame her. Emma had just dissed Kyle's football skills – who knew what the guy might do?

But to Daniel's shock, he didn't do anything except smile.

'OK,' he said. 'But I bet your girls' gymnastics team couldn't do *this* . . .'

He turned and sprinted towards his teammates. 'Howl and Prowl, guys!'

As the Beasts prepared to execute another wild play, Emma shook her head. 'These football players sure are full of themselves.' She sighed.

'That's why I prefer the more musical type,' said Debi, reaching out to give Daniel's arm a squeeze . . . with her left hand.

This set off a rapid-fire round of super loud sneezes.

'I think I'm gonna head inside,' he told Debi, when the sneezing *finally* subsided. 'I, uh . . . really need to . . .'

. . . *Get away from that nightmare of a bracelet you're wearing.*

'. . . head inside.'

Good explaining, doofus, he thought, furious with himself.

'OK,' said Debi. 'I guess I'll see you tomorrow.'

As Daniel turned to leave, he heard Kyle bark out another 'Hike!' This was soon followed by a sound that didn't require super-hearing to identify: Defensive players crashing to the ground with bone-crushing thuds.

Just as Daniel reached the school's entrance, his wolf ears picked up Emma's voice. She was telling Debi that the Pine Wood jocks certainly had a very *interesting* way of welcoming a new girl to their school.

Daniel wished it were as simple as that. Three backflips? Come on! That wasn't just over-the-top, that was over the top *of* over-the-top!

The more he thought about it, the more it seemed to Daniel that the Beasts simply *couldn't help themselves*. It was like they *had* to show off.

But why?

Chapter Four

Justin and the Beasts were heading to the Meat & Greet. Which was on Main Street. Two blocks up from where Justin was supposed to meet Riley. Kyle said they needed burgers to re-energise, and when a burger was in question there was no way to keep a wolf from that door.

If Justin stopped at the dance studio, they'd be right there with him.

On the upside, he wasn't going to be late; on the downside – like the *way* down side – there was no way he'd be able to just excuse himself from his teammates and turn into samba central without taking some pretty serious razzing.

As they passed Pine Wood Pharmacy, a window display of cold and flu remedies gave him an idea.

'*Ah-choooo!*' He made a big show of wiping his nose on his sleeve.

'Dude, use a tissue!' said Kyle – the guy Justin had once seen drop a chunk of steak, save it by flicking out his dirty football boot, then kick it back up into the air and catch it with his mouth.

'*AH . . . AHH. AHHHHHH-CHOOOO!*' Justin's follow-up fake sneeze was even fake-sloppier than the first. This time he pulled up the whole front of his shirt to fake-wipe his nose on.

'Sorry, guys. I guess I caught my brother's cold. Much as I'm craving a burger, I think I'd better just head home. I don't wanna be sick when we play Riverside next week.'

'Yeah, maybe you should,' said Kyle.

'OK, well, see ya.' Automatically, Justin raised his hand to accept Kyle's usual, palm-crushing farewell high-five. But to his surprise, Kyle gave him a look like Justin had just put lettuce on a hamburger.

'You just *sneezed* all over that hand, dude,' sneered Kyle.

'Oh, right. Sorry.'

Justin said goodbye, then ducked into the pharmacy. When the Beasts were around the corner and out of sight, he sprinted the rest of the way to the dance studio. He wound up standing beneath the sign that read MISS MIRANDA'S HOUSE OF DANCE with thirty seconds to spare!

In fact, Riley was only just arriving.

'Hi!' she said, giving him a hug. 'I hope you didn't have any trouble getting here.'

You have no idea, thought Justin, hugging her back.

As they approached the door to the wood-floored dance area, they saw an enormous bulletin board. On it was a notice about an upcoming audition for:

THE PINE WOOD TOURING DANCE TROUPE

The notice included a photo of the troupe's 'illustrious, renowned' director, Louis Gutterson – who looked a little like Albert Einstein, mixed with a great white shark – above a note asking for *'Experienced Dancers Only'*.

'Guess that leaves us out,' Justin joked. 'I never knew Pine Wood had a dance troupe.'

'I never knew Pine Wood had werewolves,' Riley whispered, giggling.

61

In addition to the photo of Louis the Dancing Genius Shark, there were class schedules, announcements for performances, lost-and-found notices about missing tap shoes, and a poster advertising an upcoming fundraiser for one of Pine Wood's most beloved local charities:

PINE WOOD CHILDREN'S HOSPITAL

FUN FOR THE WHOLE FAMILY

INCLUDING:

FOOD AND ENTERTAINMENT

GAMES AND PRIZES

SKEE-BALL TOURNAMENT

BALLROOM DANCE EXHIBITION

*COMPETITIVE DANCE CONTEST – JUDGED BY

LOUIS GUTTERSON*

AND SPECIAL CELEBRITY GUESTS

Saturday

6.00 p.m.

Someone had circled the part about the Competitive Dance Contest in red marker.

'We should totally be part of that,' said Riley.

Justin's eyes flew open in surprise. 'The Dance Contest?' They hadn't had a single lesson yet and she wanted to compete?

Riley laughed. 'Absolutely not! I meant the fundraising effort.' She gave his arm a squeeze. 'Because if this dancing idea doesn't help me get over my clumsiness, it's only a matter of time before I break a leg! When that happens, it would be wonderful to know our local hospital can afford state-of-the-art-medical equipment.'

Justin chuckled as he led her into the studio area.

The room was huge, with a gleaming wooden floor, ballet barres, and floor-to-cciling mirrors on three of the four walls. Their footsteps echoed as they made their way to the centre of the room.

Suddenly a shrill voice pierced the quiet. 'What do you think you're doing on my dance floor in street shoes?'

Startled, Justin and Riley jerked their heads towards the sound. A tall woman in a purple leotard stood in the doorway, glowering at them.

'In fact,' the woman hissed, 'what are you doing in my studio *at all*?'

'Are you Miss Miranda?' Riley asked.

The woman smiled a snake-like smile. 'What tipped you off, darling? Was it this picture of me with my name beneath it?' She pointed to a large painting on the mirror-free wall – a dark-tinted portrait in swirling oil paints. Beneath it hung a gilded plaque that read: *Miranda Malinovsky*.

'We'd like to take lessons,' Riley explained politely.

Miss Miranda gave a condescending sniff. 'I can tell just by looking at those lanky legs of yours that you have as much coordination as a three-legged rhinoceros!' She tossed her chin-length black hair and snorted. 'Your elbows look positively lethal – the fact that you made it to the centre of the studio without falling flat on your face is practically a miracle. You are obviously *not* a dancer.'

A bright pink flush crawled up Riley's neck and into her cheeks. She looked both embarrassed and angry that a total stranger – an adult! – could be so rude.

'Isn't that the point of taking classes?' Justin challenged Miranda. 'To learn?'

'I teach dance,' Miranda sniffed. 'I don't perform magic!' She waved her hand, dismissing them. 'Kindly see yourselves out!'

With that, she rose on to her toes and spun away, pirouetting past them towards the mirror-less wall.

For a moment Justin stood there, gawping after the dance teacher. He was about to try laughing it off when he saw the hurt in Riley's eyes.

'Let's get out of here,' she said, jerking her arm free from his and storming out of the studio.

Justin ran after her, pausing only long enough to grab their coats before dashing out to the sidewalk.

He was too late. In her rush, Riley hadn't noticed a patch of ice just outside the studio door; by the time Justin caught up, she'd already slipped and landed on her butt.

'Are you OK?' Justin asked, hurrying towards her.

'No,' Riley huffed. 'I just proved that nasty woman's point. Maybe I am un-teachable.'

Then Justin noticed the sign on the Pine Wood Community Centre across the street.

'I say we get a second opinion,' he said, gently helping Riley to her feet. He motioned with his chin in the direction of the sign.

Free Dance Classes Tonight

'We've come this far,' he said. 'Might as well take one more shot. It can't be any worse than Mean Madame Miranda's Mansion of Mambo, can it?'

Riley laughed. 'I suppose it can't.'

A class was just beginning when they walked into the community centre's all-purpose room. It was vast, like the dance studio, but with fewer mirrors.

The floor was already crowded with couples. They were mostly high school seniors, Justin thought. One look at the clearly experienced bunch of dancers had Riley panicking again.

'Let's just go,' she whispered. 'I'm sure the teacher won't notice if we slip out.'

'Relax,' said Justin. 'We'll be fine.'

Now the instructor stepped to the front of the room. Like Miranda, she was tall and elegant. She wore a simple black leotard with black leggings, and her long, red hair was in a knot at the back of her neck.

Unlike Miranda, she had a very friendly smile.

'As you all know,' she began sweetly, 'we've been working very hard in preparation for the dance contest at the hospital fundraiser. Our presence there is sure to bring in a great many donations, which would be wonderful.' She paused, and Justin thought her eyes grew a little more serious. 'But I can't stress enough how *very* important it is that our school makes a triumphant showing in the contest. You are all very talented, and it is my sincere hope is that we will sweep the competition, taking home the first, second and third place medals.'

Riley frowned. 'She has some pretty high expectations,' she whispered. 'I don't think we're ready for such a super-demanding instructor.'

It was at that moment that the super-demanding instructor noticed the young couple at the back of the group.

'Oh,' she said, smiling. 'I didn't see you come in.'

'We were late,' said Justin. 'Sorry.'

'I'm Miss Samantha. I run the community centre's dance programme.'

'I'm Justin, and this is Riley.'

'Nice to meet you both.' Miss Samantha gave them a hopeful look. 'Have you two had much dancing experience?'

Riley sighed. 'More like none.'

'Beginners?' Miss Samantha made a

disappointed *tsk*. 'That's a shame.'

'Why is it a shame?' Justin asked. 'We don't mind if we're a little behind.'

'Well, that's certainly the right attitude.' Miss Samantha's eyes were warm. 'Ordinarily, I'd love to have you join our class. But with the contest coming up, I'm afraid I need to focus on my more advanced students, as they will be competing soon. Maybe if you came back after the contest –'

'That's not a problem,' Riley blurted, sounding relieved. 'Thanks anyway.'

She took Justin's hand and began backing off the floor.

But this time, he was the one to clutch her hand in an extra-firm grip. 'Wait.'

'Justin, you heard what Miss Samantha said.'

He had, of course. But there was something about this teacher – the Anti-Miranda – that made him think she'd understand. He took a deep breath and faced the instructor.

'Miss Samantha, you have no idea how much this means to us. We really want to learn to dance. Even if you won't be able to work with us directly, even if we can't compete, it'll be really helpful just to be part of your class. I'm afraid if you send us away now, neither of us will have the guts to come back.'

Miss Samantha considered for a long moment. Finally, she nodded.

'All right,' she said. 'For now, just do the best you can. And – more importantly – have fun!'

'Thanks,' said Justin. He found a place directly behind a couple who looked like they knew what they were doing. Riley took her place beside him as Miss Samantha started class with some warm-up exercises.

This isn't too hard, Justin thought.

But when Miss Samantha had them move diagonally across the floor in pairs, things began to look bleak. While the other students *quietly* shifted their weight from foot to foot, Riley's every step made a sound that fell somewhere between a *thud* and a *thwack*.

And, worst of all, Riley and Justin just could *not* get themselves in sync.

When Justin moved left, Riley leaned right; he went forward when she went back – if he zigged, she zagged.

Finally, Miss Samantha turned off the music. She gave Riley a long, thoughtful look. But just as she was about to speak, Riley held up her hand.

'You don't have to say it,' she sighed. 'I know I'm hopeless.'

'I wasn't going to say that,' Miss Samantha said gently. 'I was going to say, you must learn to trust your body.'

Riley shook her head. 'Trust it to do what? Endanger everyone else on the dance floor?'

'Find your partner's rhythm,' Samantha continued, 'and let him find yours.'

'That would be much easier if I actually *had* any rhythm,' Riley said.

'A dance,' said Miss Samantha, looking at them intently, 'is really just a relationship set to music. It's about being patient, and being able to read your partner's moods and motions.' A tiny grin curled up the corners of her mouth. 'Am I correct in assuming that you two are boyfriend and girlfriend?'

To answer, Justin and Riley blushed.

'Good,' said Samantha. 'Then I have the perfect solution.'

She crossed the room in three long, elegant strides and dug in her dance bag. Seconds later she returned, holding a little pinkish blob that

Justin recognised as one his favourite childhood playthings: Phunny Putty. He and Daniel used to spend hours moulding and stretching the sticky stuff.

'Riley, do you trust Justin?' Samantha asked.

'Completely.' Riley didn't hesitate.

'Excellent.' Samantha pinched off a piece of the plastic-y putty and stretched it until it was a thin string about six inches in length. She gave one end of the springy-but-fragile thread to Riley and the other end to Justin.

'The idea is to keep in tune with each other,' Samantha explained. 'This string will help you do that. Your goal is to move around the room as carefully as you can – the putty will snap if one of you moves more than a step too far from the other.'

Justin wanted to tell the teacher she didn't have to worry about that. He'd spent most of his life working up the nerve to get close to Riley; the last thing he wanted to do was step *away* from her.

'Everyone else, work on your dances for the competition. Riley, Justin, keep that plastic putty in one piece.'

Miss Samantha motioned to one of the other students to turn the music back on.

'Ready?' said Justin.

'Ready,' said Riley.

As the music filled the room, they walked slowly, concentrating on the putty strung between them. At first, it strained as they misjudged each other's moves, but soon they began moving in unison, the string steady between them.

'I think I'm getting the hang of it,' Riley whispered, sounding pleased.

Just then a harsh laugh could be heard over the music.

The sound was so jarring that Riley missed a step. Justin saw it coming like one of Kyle Hunter's long passes, and managed to offset her mistake with a graceful glide. His eyes immediately shot to the plastic string which, thankfully, had remained unbroken. But when he looked up, he saw that all the dancers were staring at Miss Miranda, who stood like a giant purple snake in the doorway. Her condescending glare went straight to the Phunny Putty stretched so fragilely between Justin and Riley.

'Well, look who's still using that ridiculous "Trust String" exercise,' she snickered, shaking her head disdainfully. 'Our old dance instructor despised that silly trick. But then again, Samantha, I suppose I could see how someone with your lack of talent would have to rely on gimmicks.'

Samantha, who had her back to the entrance,

stayed focused on the dancers and did not say a word.

Now Miranda held up a poster, which Justin recognised as the one for the hospital fundraiser.

'I just wanted to point out that, in addition to the dance competition, there's going to be a ballroom dance *exhibition* as well. Judging by the level of – *ahem* – "ability" in this room, I'd suggest you all set your sights on *that* instead. No point in embarrassing yourselves by competing against *my* students.'

Finally, Miss Samantha spoke. 'This is a private class, Miranda,' she said calmly. 'I would appreciate it if you'd leave.'

'Gladly,' Miranda trilled. 'I was just popping in to scout out the competition, but I don't see any here.' She laughed at her own joke, then flounced out the door.

Aside from the music that continued to play

softly, the class fell silent. No one moved, except Samantha, who turned to flash a forced smile. 'Keep dancing, everyone,' she said. 'Remember, we *have* to win that contest.'

'I think she's upset,' Riley whispered.

Justin nodded, but he was distracted by the idea that was forming in his mind.

'Please don't worry about Miranda,' Samantha continued. 'We danced together when we were young and, well . . . let's just say we won't be doing a *pas de deux* any time soon.' She pointed to Justin and Riley and gave them a big smile. 'But, speaking of duets, look at our new students! They made it all the way around the room without breaking the string.'

There was a ripple of applause from the other couples.

'I'd say that proves you're a great teacher,' said Riley, as Miss Samantha beamed at them.

'And it proves that Riley has a lot more coordination than she gives herself credit for,' Justin added.

When class was over, Miss Samantha came over to Justin and Riley and put her arms around their shoulders. 'I'm glad you convinced me to let you stay. You did wonderfully.'

'Thanks,' said Justin, grinning. 'Maybe tomorrow we can take things up a notch and work on our polka skills.'

Miss Samantha laughed. 'I don't see any reason why not. I have a feeling you two are going to be wonderful dancers.'

'I was thinking the same thing,' said Justin. 'Which is why Riley and I are going to dance at the fundraiser next week.'

Riley had been smiling so much during class that Justin was not prepared for the horrified look she was giving him now. Perhaps sensing that her new students needed to have a *private* discussion, Miss Samantha quickly congratulated them once more, then excused herself to pack up her things.

When they were alone, Riley started shaking her head as if she'd just been asked if she wanted to bungee jump using Phunny Putty. 'No, Justin. No, no ... No. Just ... No ...'

'Don't worry,' Justin said, putting his hands on her shoulders. 'It can't be any harder than simultaneously running a book donation drive for a Guatemalan orphanage *and* circulating a petition to upgrade the school library's computer card catalogue – and that, if I remember correctly, is exactly what you did last week.'

'You forgot "overseeing the re-tiling of the

girls locker room showers"',' Riley murmured.

'That's my point,' said Justin, giving her a gentle shake. 'Riley Carter does not fear challenges – challenges fear Riley Carter.'

She grinned in spite of herself. 'I don't know . . .' She pulled away and turned to face herself in the mirror. 'Me? Dance in public?'

Justin wished she could see what *he* saw in that reflection: the most perfect girl on the planet.

'Petitions and sit-ins come naturally to me.' Riley sighed. 'But anything involving grace and coordination? Not so much. Besides . . .' Her eyes met his in the mirror. 'Do you want your teammates to know you've been waltzing in your spare time?'

Justin rolled his eyes. 'The Beasts aren't exactly the community service type. Unless the hospital gives out free T-bone steaks – raw ones – I'd say it's a safe bet they will be no-shows.'

Riley giggled.

'I know you can do this,' he said, trying not to sound *too* much like Coach Johnston talking to his *human* Defensive players when they came up against a better-than-average opponent. 'You and I are going to prove it by dancing up a storm at that fundraiser.'

They were smiling at each other when something outside the dance studio window caught Justin's eye . . . a flash of motion. He told himself it was nothing. *Coming from a Lupine family, you tend to think you see werewolves everywhere.*

But even though Justin knew it made no sense, he could not shake the feeling that he had seen . . . *fur*.

Chapter Five

One of Daniel's favourite things about being part of an actual, for-real official couple was the standing lunch date he had with Debi every day. It was great to know that he didn't have to panic about asking her if she wanted to sit with him – because he knew the answer would always be 'Yes'. They even had a 'usual table' that they shared with Justin and Riley.

Unfortunately, today, they were also sharing it with the Beasts.

Across the table, Justin gave him an apologetic

look. Daniel shrugged in response. He actually didn't mind the Beasts all that much, especially now that he and Justin were no longer keeping secrets from them. The football players knew that it was Daniel, not Justin, who was the Lupine. And Daniel had to admit, it was pretty awesome the way they still treated Justin as one of their own. They were good guys, but still . . . Daniel wanted to talk to Justin about his new 'hobby' – the new hobby Justin almost certainly didn't want the Beasts finding out about.

'How did the, um . . .' Daniel paused, wondering how to discuss the topic without the Beasts figuring it out '. . . *extra training session* go last night, Justin?'

Justin had a look of happy surprise when he answered, 'Really well. And Riley was great.'

'Dude,' said Chris Jordan, using his sleeve to wipe a trickle of burger juice from his chin, 'did I just hear Dan-o say something about extra training?'

Justin nodded. 'You know me. I like to take it to the max.'

'But what did you mean about Riley? Don't tell me you were training with a *girl*!'

'Who do you think created his training chart?' said Riley easily. 'Actually, I prepared an entire spreadsheet, outlining the proper proportion of aerobic activity to resistance-training exercises, with a side bar about adequate hydration levels.'

Daniel bit back a laugh. Riley was covering for Justin, but she had actually created the chart. Daniel had seen it.

Kyle laughed. 'Way to go, Packer. You didn't just find yourself a girlfriend, you got a personal trainer.'

'Yeah, well, that kind of thing comes easy to her,' Justin agreed, throwing Riley a wink. 'She "danced" her way right through it.'

'Maybe you guys should consider getting girlfriends,' said Debi. 'Boys like to show off when there are girls around,' she added, giving the Beasts a teasing look. 'You ought to know. After all, you were practically killing yourselves at practice yesterday to impress Emma the new girl.'

The Beasts looked at the table, the floor — anywhere but at Debi. *I guess even* they *agree their behaviour on Monday was weird*, Daniel thought.

'Whatcha' readin'?' Kyle asked quickly, pointing at Debi's magazine. He seemed keen to change the subject.

Debi tossed her head. 'Oh, nothing special,' she said in an off-hand tone. 'Just an article about an actual Hollywood movie shoot coming to Pine Wood.'

'What?!' gasped Riley, leaning closer to read the article.

'What movie?' Chris demanded.

'And are they looking for great-looking, charismatic, athletic locals to be extras?' Ed Yancey asked through a mouthful of burger. 'Sign me up!'

'Me too,' said Caleb Devlin. 'I wouldn't mind hanging around with a bunch of gorgeous starlets.'

'So, is anyone famous in this flick?' Kyle asked.

In reply, Riley let out an ear-piercing squeal that startled Daniel so badly he dropped his sandwich.

'Jackson Caulfield!' Riley cried. 'Jackson Caulfield is coming to Pine Wood to film *Eternal Sunset*!'

'Can you believe it?' Debi sighed. 'Jando is going to be right here in our town!'

'What's a Jando?' Calcb asked.

'It's not a "what", it's a "who",' Debi explained. 'Actually, two "whos".'

'Did you say, "yoo hoos"?' Daniel asked, confused.

'No,' Debi giggled. 'Jando is the nickname for Jackson and his girlfriend, Olivia Abbott. It's a combination of their initials. J and O. Which spells out "Jando".'

'Oh.' Daniel thought that was kind of cool. He'd already thought of ones for himself and Debi, but couldn't decide between 'Debinel' and 'Danbi'.

'That's gonna be an amazing movie,' Chris said. '*Eternal Sunset* was a totally awesome book. Especially the chapter where the vam–'

He trailed off, realising that the table had gone silent.

'Uh, I mean . . .' Chris gulped hard, his cheeks turning pink. 'That's what my big sister told me when *she* read it.'

Nice save, Daniel thought holding back a

laugh. Then he sneezed, ruffling the pages of the magazine which Debi was now holding (with her *left* hand) right under his nose.

'See?' she said. 'This is a picture of Jando. It's a candid shot taken when they first met in Franklin Grove. Notice anything interesting about Olivia's outfit?'

Daniel sniffled, examining the picture. Olivia, a dark haired girl with a nice smile, was standing beside the blond-haired, square-jawed Jackson. He was decked out in trendy Hollywood threads, but she was wearing a pink-and-white cheerleading uniform.

Why does that look familiar?

Now he remembered: Debi had been wearing the exact same uniform in one of the photos in the Morgans' house. She had been a cheerleader on the same squad as Olivia.

'I forgot you knew her back in Franklin Grove,'

Daniel said. He couldn't help being impressed by the image of his girlfriend going to school with a movie star. Of course, Debi was amazing all on her own. If anything, Olivia – the O in Jando – should consider herself lucky to know Debi . . . the 'Morg' half of 'Morgacker'.

OK, that definitely needs work.

'We were squad-mates,' Debi clarified. 'It'll be nice to see her again when she comes to film here.'

A snort of disbelief came from the next table. Daniel turned to see Mackenzie eyeing Debi. 'Oh, *please*! Do you want us to believe that you and Olivia Abbott are besties?'

Debi frowned slightly. 'I never said that. I only said we were friendly.'

Mackenzie rolled her eyes. 'Friendly, huh? Well, if you guys were so *friendly*, does that mean you have a ton of super-secret gossip about her and Jackson? Like, do you know the inside story behind their whole romance?'

Debi lifted one shoulder in a dainty shrug. 'I know the same story everyone else does,' she said sweetly. 'Jackson met Olivia while filming *The Groves* and she totally stole his heart.'

'Well, if you ask me,' said Mackenzie with a flip of her hair, 'this "Jando" nonsense is getting *really* old. Maybe while Jackson's here in Pine Wood he'll find someone he likes a whole lot better. Like me.'

Daniel almost choked on his mouthful of soda. Was their head cheerleader really that delusional? Did she really think the movie rags would be writing articles about 'Mackson' or 'Jackenzie' or 'Bartfield' anytime soon?

'Maybe we shouldn't get our hopes up about the movie coming here,' Mackenzie said sourly. 'The producers might choose another location when they hear about that dangerous wild dog roaming our town.'

At that comment, Kyle just about gagged on his last bite of burger. Ed and Chris began sputtering, too, and Caleb coughed so hard that ginger beer came shooting out of his nose.

Daniel's senses went on alert so quickly he had to tug down his sleeves to fend off any sudden fur-sproutage. Why were the Beasts freaking out? Did *they* know something about this 'wild dog'?

Is it a werewolf?

Debi laughed. 'Oh, I wouldn't worry about that. It's probably just Mrs Hammerstein's dog wandering around.'

Justin and Daniel exchanged looks.

'You're probably right, Debi,' said Riley, before Mackenzie could ask who Mrs Hammerstein even *was*. 'But the Hollywood people won't know that.'

Daniel was beginning to wish the problem actually *was* old Mrs Hammerstein and her mutt.

Just then, Daniel felt Justin nudge him and, when he turned, his brother was slipping a napkin across the table towards him.

At first Daniel only saw a series of yellow squiggles; it took him a moment to realise that while he'd been distracted by the Beasts' gasping and coughing, Justin had used a mustard packet to squirt out a message on the napkin:

Last night on Main Street

Daniel frowned. What did that mean? Justin must have run out of mustard before he could finish the note.

A moment later a second napkin came scooting across the lunch table with the rest of the message written in ketchup:

I saw FUR

Daniel stared at his brother with wide eyes. Justin gave him a quick nod.

'Oh, man, this is gonna be a problem,' Daniel muttered.

Debi overheard him but, fortunately, she thought he was talking to her. 'You might be right. If the producers think it's dangerous here, they could move the shoot to somewhere else. And that's a double bummer, because it says here –' she pointed to the last paragraph of the article – 'that since Winifred Peters is acting as special consultant on the film, she'll be travelling with the cast and crew. I was totally hoping to meet her in person.'

'Who's Winifred Peters?' Caleb asked. 'Another movie star?'

'She's the author of *Eternal Sunset*,' said Chris.

'Count Vira is her pen name. Don't you know anything?'

'Enough about books – books are lame,' said Kyle, picking up the last chunk of nearly-raw burger from his plate. 'Kyle going long,' he announced, cocking his arm back and launching the burger-chunk across the cafeteria.

Stunned, the rest of the cafeteria watched as the quarterback hopped out of his seat and began leaping from table to table in pursuit of his flying meal. At the last table, he turned, tilted his head back and caught the burger chunk in his mouth. Smiling broadly as he chewed, he swept a low bow to his staring schoolmates.

The Beasts howled and clapped and stamped their feet, while the rest of the student body responded with a confused round of applause.

'Man,' said Justin, 'that kinda gives a new meaning to the term "fast food".'

Daniel was about to reply when he noticed that Emma Sharpe, the new girl he and Debi had met yesterday, had just stepped out of the lunch line and was walking across the cafeteria with her tray.

Mackenzie noticed, too; she was glaring at Emma with narrowed eyes. 'Do you think those blonde streaks are natural,' she seethed, 'or just a really intense dye-job?'

Daniel didn't know and he didn't care. Right now, Emma's blonde-and-light-brown locks were the least of his worries.

Because Kyle had turned his triumphant grin in Emma's direction, before dismounting the table with a double somersault. He landed smoothly, before swaggering back to his own seat as stunned silence fell over the cafeteria.

To make matters worse, the other Beasts had shifted into hyper-mode, too. Chris tried to use his fork to catapult a French fry into his mouth, which resulted in a faceful of ketchup for Ed.

'Sorry,' said Chris. 'I was aiming for my own mouth.'

'How about *I* aim for your mouth?' Ed snarled, balling up his fist.

Luckily, Principal Caine, who happened to be on lunch duty, made her way over to their table. She gave Ed a stern look and he backed off. Then the principal wagged a finger at Kyle. 'Mr Hunter, kindly save those acrobatics for the football field.'

Kyle gave a sheepish nod, but when the principal had drifted past, he began throwing 'playful punches' to Caleb's shoulder, which a laughing Caleb threw right back.

Daniel had heard quieter drum solos.

His gaze was plucked from the Beasts when he noticed Emma drawing closer to their table.

The nearer she got, the more edgy the Beasts seemed to become. Showing off for the new girl was bad enough on a wide-open football field, but in a confined space like the school cafeteria, it was a disaster waiting to happen!

And why is Emma walking right up to our table as if this is totally normal? Daniel wondered, feeling a sudden stab of panic as he realised that she was probably going to sit down with them. After all, it was her first week and Debi and Daniel were probably the only people she actually knew.

If the Beasts were punching each other with Emma halfway across the room, what would they do if she was less than a foot from them?

Just as Emma reached Debi's end of the table, Principal Caine called out, 'Miss Sharpe, may I speak with you for a moment? I'd love to hear how you're settling in.'

Emma gave Debi a smile and a shrug, and

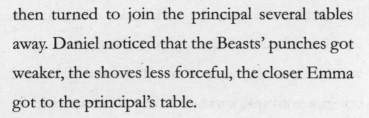

then turned to join the principal several tables away. Daniel noticed that the Beasts' punches got weaker, the shoves less forceful, the closer Emma got to the principal's table.

'Ahem . . .'

Daniel dragged his gaze away from where Emma was sitting with Principal Caine, only to find Debi looking at him with a confused expression.

His heart lurched. She must have been watching him watch Emma that whole time! Was she afraid that he'd been checking out the new girl?

Before he could explain himself, the bell rang. Riley popped out of her seat and took Debi's arm.

'Let's go to the library and check online to see if there have been any more dog sightings,' she said. 'I don't want Winifred Peters' visit to be cancelled.'

Debi gave Daniel one more curious glance before following Riley out of the cafeteria.

He figured it was just as well that he hadn't had a chance to speak to her. After all, what could he have said?

Don't worry – I wasn't looking at Emma because I'm interested *in her. I was just interested in why the Beasts go berserk every time she's within a fifty metre radius.*

That sounded crazy, even to him.

Daniel had no idea what was going on around here, but he was going to have to find out fast – before Debi noticed he was being weird and jumped to the wrong conclusion.

Chapter Six

Daniel tore open the wrapping on Debi's gift and opened the box. He threw the necklace to the end of his bed.

What had he been thinking? Seashells were something little kids collected in plastic buckets, they were *not* something you made into a necklace and gave your girlfriend as a birthday present.

He would have to find something better.

He'd just picked up the necklace again when Justin came in, grimy and sweaty from football practice.

'Don't you have dance class?' Daniel asked.

'Not until later,' said Justin, scooting into their shared bathroom and turning on the shower. He popped back into Daniel's room and gave him a puzzled look.

'Was it my imagination,' said Justin, 'or were the Beasts acting weird at lunch today?'

'I think it has something to do with Emma,' said Daniel, as he put the gift box back into his nightstand drawer.

'The new girl?'

Daniel nodded. 'Remember when we were watching practice yesterday, and the Beasts were showing off? I think they started right as she showed up. And today, they were perfectly normal – well, as normal as those guys ever are – right up until Emma walked into the cafeteria.'

As Justin considered this, a cloud of steam wafted in from the bathroom. 'OK, so maybe it *is* Emma,' he said, disappearing into the mist. 'But why are they acting so crazy? It's not like they've never seen a girl before.'

'That's the point,' Daniel called towards the bathroom. 'It's almost like they can't help themselves when she's around. I'm beginning to think it's some kind of wolf-thing.'

From the bathroom, Daniel heard the shower door opening and closing.

'If it's a wolf-thing,' Justin gurgled from under the stream of hot water, 'why don't *you* act like a Lupine lunatic whenever she's around?'

'Good question,' Daniel shouted so Justin would hear him above the sound of the shower. 'Maybe it's a jock-thing?'

'OK,' Justin sputtered, 'then why aren't *I* acting like a jock jerk?'

Daniel flopped back on the bed. *That* was a good question. Was there something wrong with his brother the jock? Or something wrong with

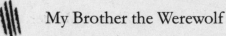

Daniel the werewolf? He wasn't even sure he wanted to know the answer.

A half-hour later, Justin called Daniel into the living room, where he was waiting for Mr Carter to pick him up and drive him and Riley to the community centre.

'Do me a favour, bro,' Justin said. 'I need you to tell me what you think of my cha-cha-cha.'

'Your what-what—*what?*'

Justin laughed. 'It's a dance. You know . . . one, two, cha-cha-cha; three, four, cha-cha-cha . . .'

'Five, six . . . *are you kidding?* You really want *my* opinion?'

'You're musical. I wanna be sure I don't look like a dope.'

Daniel figured that had to be impossible when

doing something with a name like the 'cha-cha-cha', but the look on Justin's face made him keep it to himself. 'Fine. Let's see what you've got.'

'OK, but remember, we've only had one class so far.' Justin hit the play button on his music player, took a deep breath . . . and started dancing!

Not that it was much of a dance. Basically, Justin just kept stepping from one foot to the other, putting his right foot in front, then shaking his hips – 'cha-cha-cha' – then putting his left foot out and marching in place – 'cha-cha-cha' – before doing the whole thing over again in the opposite order.

Their dad popped his head into the living room. 'Am I crazy or do I hear someone playing a cha-cha-cha?'

Daniel nodded towards Justin, who was really into it now. He was turning and wiggling like someone with a bad case of poison ivy. At least he was doing it in time to the music.

'Wow, he's really in the zone,' Mr Packer observed.

'Better him than me,' quipped Daniel. 'Hey, Dad, can I talk to you for a minute?'

'Sure.' Mr Packer stepped into the living room and perched on the arm of the sofa. 'About what?'

'Well . . . about boys and girls.'

'Oh, uh . . .' Mr Packer went red in the face, and over the bright hue in his cheeks Daniel noticed a prickly stubble of wolf fur popping out.

'Don't you think you might want to talk to Mom about this . . . uh . . . this particular . . . topic?'

'Not *that* kind of thing,' Daniel explained quickly. 'It's a Lupine thing.'

'Ah.' Mr Packer relaxed, his stubbly cheeks smoothing over. 'Then I'm your guy.'

Over by the window, Justin continued to swivel his hips.

Daniel forced himself to ignore his twin. 'You know Justin's teammates have always been a bunch of show offs, right? Well, lately they've really been pushing things to the limit.'

'Step *up*, cha-cha-cha . . .'

Dad folded his arms. 'Really?'

Daniel nodded. 'Yeah, and what I figured out today is that there's a trigger for their actions. A girl. A *new* girl.'

Mr Packer's eyebrows shot up, but he didn't say anything.

'Lean *back*, cha-cha-cha . . .'

'So what do you think, Dad?' Daniel prodded, noticing that his father seemed lost in thought.

'It's probably nothing,' Mr Packer mumbled.

It doesn't look like nothing, Daniel thought, feeling his fangs tingle with worry. He stepped closer to his father, trying not to show that worry – trying to look his most mature – as he said: 'No, there's something. Is it something I should know about?'

'There's some tension in our community, Daniel,' Mr Packer sighed. 'Tension . . . and worry.'

'And *turn* now, cha-cha-cha . . . let's *cross* now . . .'

Daniel had to fight the urge to toss one of the couch pillows at Justin's head. 'Worry about what?' he asked his dad.

'Something strange has been happening,' Mr Packer explained, his tone dark. 'Have you heard about these sightings of "big dogs"?' When Daniel nodded, his dad continued: 'People have been calling the animal control officers about a "large, light-coloured animal" they've seen roaming the area. Some of the elder wolves are wondering if it's a lone Lupine.'

Daniel was afraid of this. 'Could it be one of the Beasts acting up, sneaking out at night to cause trouble? They've seemed pretty "pumped" lately . . . Kyle was doing somersaults in the lunch room. Maybe he snuck out when they weren't looking . . .'

Mr Packer thought about this for a moment. 'I don't know,' he said. 'Lupine parents keep *very* strict watch on their children.'

Across the room, Justin did a half spin. 'One, *two*, cha-cha-*what*?' He almost tripped over his own feet.

Daniel shared his twin's shock. 'How "strict"?'

'Well, you know,' said their dad with a shrug. 'We're the parents of young Lupines who mix and mingle with humans every day. It's sensible to stay informed.'

'Yeah, but-but-but . . .' Justin stammered, the cha-cha-cha completely forgotten.

Mr Packer held up his hands. 'There's no *spying*,' he said. 'With our enhanced senses, we'd probably find out everything anyway. That's not the point – the point is the community still has a problem to straighten out.'

'What would be so bad about a lone wolf coming to town, anyway?' Daniel asked. 'Maybe he's just looking for a new pack to join . . . Maybe he . . . What?' He noticed that his dad was staring at the floor, deep in thought.

'It might not be a "he",' said Mr Packer.

Daniel's mouth had dropped open and Justin was blinking in amazement.

'But I remember you telling me,' said Justin, 'there was no such thing as a female werewolf. So how can there be a . . . a . . . wolf-*ette* running around Lycan Point?'

The twins' dad smiled at Justin's phrase, then seemed to correct himself. 'I know I say this a lot, but this time I really mean it – what I'm about to tell you is a *huge* secret. I never said there was no such thing as female werewolves, I only said that they were *very* rare. In fact, as far as we know, only a handful of she-wolves are born each century.'

The twins took a minute to let this sink in.

'So what are she-wolves like?' Daniel asked.

Their dad scratched at his cheek, where tufts of fur had begun to pop up. 'They are faster, stronger and more powerful than male wolves could ever hope to be.'

The twins shared a befuddled glance. 'Faster?' Daniel frowned.

Justin's confused expression was one that Daniel usually only saw when they had a pop-quiz in their Physics class. 'Stronger?'

'And in command of *much* greater power,' Mr Packer confirmed.

Daniel gulped, imagining how well this

information would go over with the Beasts. He pictured a female wolf in a cheerleading skirt, towering over Kyle Hunter, and clobbering him over the head with a pom-pom.

Part of him would not have minded seeing *that*.

'Females turn "full wolf" at a much younger age than their male counterparts,' their dad explained. 'This makes them incredibly powerful.'

At that moment, a car horn sounded in the driveway. 'That's Riley and her dad,' said Justin, smoothing his hair. 'I gotta go, but Daniel can fill me in later.' He was halfway to the hallway when he turned back. 'Dad, I just remembered – I thought I saw something furry down on Main Street last night. Should I keep an eye out to see if he – I mean, *she* – comes back tonight?'

'Yes,' Mr Packer said sombrely. 'If she does . . . be careful.'

Justin nodded, then hurried out the door.

Daniel noticed that his dad looked more upset than ever. 'It's bad enough she's been running about in wolf form at the Point,' he muttered. 'Now she's taken to the streets.'

'I think I sensed her at that fancy French restaurant a few nights ago,' Daniel informed his father. 'I guess she doesn't care much about the rules.'

'It looks that way,' muttered Mr Packer, dragging a hand down his face in frustration. 'I've never met a she-wolf, but according to folklore, they tend to be reckless in their youth. I suppose it's because there are so few of them that they never have a chance to develop a pack mentality.'

Now something occurred to Daniel. 'How would I know if it was a she-wolf, and not a, uh ... *he*-wolf?'

'By their fur,' Mr Packer answered. He rolled up his sleeve and sprouted a thick mass of dark fur, just over his forearm – completely by choice. For Daniel, who was still trying to keep his accidental turning under control, this was a pretty remarkable skill.

'See how dark my fur is?' said Mr Packer.

Daniel nodded. Every wolf he knew, teen and adult alike, had fur in that same sable-and-grey color.

'I've heard that she-wolves are much lighter,' Mr Packer explained. 'They're a frostier brown, and often have streaks running through their fur that are almost platinum blonde. And those colours match the descriptions non-Lupines have given of the "Big Dog" they may or may not have seen.' Then he grinned as he rolled the sleeve back down. 'But the glimpses have been so fleeting, we don't know for sure that anyone's seen a wolf at all, much less a she-wolf. We're probably all overreacting.'

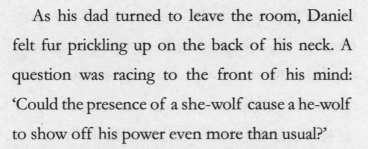

As his dad turned to leave the room, Daniel felt fur prickling up on the back of his neck. A question was racing to the front of his mind: 'Could the presence of a she-wolf cause a he-wolf to show off his power even more than usual?'

Mr Packer stopped in the doorway, turning to look back at Daniel. 'Absolutely,' he said. 'It's instinctive. It would be in his nature to try to earn her admiration. And this is a problem, because the more a wolf declares himself in his efforts to impress the she-wolf, the more he risks exposure of the whole wolf community. But, again –' His dad smiled, trying to look calm and casual. 'We don't know for sure that that's what's going on.'

When his dad was gone, Daniel sat and thought for a long time.

The Beasts had started going off the rails the minute Emma, the new girl, had shown up. Emma, with her streaky blonde highlights.

But Emma seemed immune to *their* beastly charms. They might have been trying to impress her, but she seemed completely uninterested in them. Plus, Daniel — who was just as much a wolf as Kyle and the others — had no desire to tumble and flip when she was near him.

It wasn't adding up.

So maybe these sightings had nothing to do with Emma Sharpe. Maybe the she-wolf scampering around town was someone — or some*thing* — else entirely.

Chapter Seven

On Wednesday, Kyle cancelled captain's practice. The Defensive squad was happy to have the afternoon off.

The Beasts, though, were on a mission.

For the second time that week, Justin found himself in the middle of a Beast pack. But this time they weren't going on a burger run.

They were heading to Lycan Point.

'Are you guys sure you wouldn't rather go to the Meat & Greet?' Justin asked.

'Maybe later,' said Kyle. 'Right now I want to see for myself what all these "big dog" sightings are about. If there *is* some mangy old mutt roaming around, who better than us to scare it away?'

'If we don't get rid of this canine trespasser, we might lose out on having a movie filmed in our town,' Chris added.

'You guys *do* remember I'm not an actual Beast, right?' said Justin.

'We're a team,' Kyle insisted.

'Right,' said Ed, giving Justin a friendly – but bone-jarring – pat on the shoulder. 'Whatever *we* do, you do, Packer. And whatever *you* do, we do.'

I don't see any of you doing the cha-cha-cha, Justin thought.

Which reminded him: he was supposed to meet Riley for another dance class with Miss Samantha.

This meant he *really* had to find a way to escape.

The tall shaggy pines of Lycan Point were in view now, and the Beasts seemed to be on high alert. Chris was sniffing the air, Ed was letting out anxious little whines, and Caleb was eyeing the ground for paw prints.

Then Kyle became perfectly still. His wolf ears emerged – long, pointy and set far back on the top of his head, their hairy tips twitching.

'Did you guys hear that?' he snarled, tilting his head.

Chris's own wolf ears pitched forward. 'Yeah.'

The others snorted and whimpered their agreement.

'Well, I didn't hear anything,' Justin said, 'because, as I might have mentioned, I don't have that whole Lupine thing going for me. Maybe it's better if I head back to town and get out of your way.'

Kyle's answer was a half-furry paw clamping down hard around Justin's forearm. 'Let's run!' he growled, nearly jerking Justin off his feet as he bolted towards the trees.

An eerie howl went up from the group as the wolves took off at top speed. There was nothing for Justin to do but run along with them.

Thwummppfff!

Kyle stopped so quickly that Justin crashed into his back and bounced off like a basketball, tumbling several feet.

Colliding with one of these giant tree trunks probably would have hurt less, he thought, blinking away the blur in his eyes.

'Hear that?' Kyle growled, angling his head. He flung a furry arm outwards, pointing one long claw. 'This way!'

Justin's vision cleared just in time for him to catch a glimpse of something darting through the trees, about twenty yards off. The werewolves moved as one, yipping and snarling as they chased the mysterious flash. Justin clambered to his feet and struggled to keep up.

120

Whatever it was they were in pursuit of had left even the werewolves for dust!

Justin stopped running, gasping for breath. He leaned against a huge boulder to await their return. He knew they wouldn't catch it . . . *or her.*

He was still panting when, minutes later, he heard them crashing through the trees.

'What happened?' Justin asked. 'Did you lose –' He almost said 'her', but caught himself in time. '– it?' he finished.

'Yeah, we lost it,' Chris mumbled. 'And it's all Caleb's fault!'

Caleb's eyes widened. 'Why is it *my* fault?'

'Because you should have taken the left flank,' Kyle snarled. 'You're a wide receiver!'

'This is a dog-hunt, not a football game,' Caleb snorted. 'Besides, you're the quarterback, so what were you doing leading from the front?'

Now Ed was shinnying up the trunk of a dead

pine. 'Maybe I can spot that pesky pooch from up here,' he called down.

The other Beasts immediately followed Ed's lead and began scampering up trees as well.

'I bet I can get higher than you, Devlin!' Kyle yipped.

'No chance!' Caleb yapped back.

'Dare you to jump from that tree to that rock outcropping near the ridge!' Chris taunted.

The one-upmanship continued for another few minutes; they were so involved in their squabbling, Justin figured they had quit looking for the 'dog', but the adrenaline of the 'hunt' was still making them want to show off.

'Let's see who can howl loud enough to start an avalanche,' Kyle suggested.

'No!' Justin cried.

From their perches, the Beasts glared down at him.

'I think you guys should come down from the trees right now!' Justin told them.

'Why?' Kyle demanded.

'Think about it,' Justin said. 'With all the big dog rumours going around, people are on the lookout for strange things happening. I'm pretty sure a bunch of wolfy-looking football players climbing trees is going to set off alarm bells!'

Kyle considered this. 'The last thing we need is somebody calling the cops on us. Everybody down.'

Justin watched as his teammates exited the trees as if they were performing in the Olympic high-diving competition.

Two half gainers, a double backflip and one inward twist later, all the Beasts were on the ground.

'I don't sense anything now,' Chris said through a yawn. 'Maybe we scared it away.'

'Let's hope so,' said Ed, rubbing his eyes. 'I'm outta here. I need to go home and catch some Zs.'

'Me too,' said Kyle, whose eyes were now drooping with exhaustion. 'This stinks. I was planning to swing by the amusement arcade to practise for the skee-ball contest, but I'm totally wiped out.'

Justin froze, wondering: *Where have I heard about a skee-ball contest?*

'Don't worry about it, dude,' said a very sleepy-looking Caleb. 'You've still got a few days to practise before the fundraiser.'

Ding! Ding! Ding!

Not only were alarm bells ringing, red lights were now flashing in Justin's head. He'd read about the skee-ball contest on the poster for the fundraiser . . . the same fundraiser where he and Riley would be dancing on Saturday night!

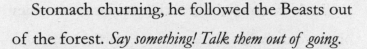

Stomach churning, he followed the Beasts out of the forest. *Say something! Talk them out of going.*

He forced a laugh. 'Dude, why would you subject yourself to the torture of some dorky fundraiser, just to play a little skee-ball?'

'Because,' said Kyle, 'there's a prize. I like prizes. Plus, I happen to rule at skee-ball. I like ruling at things.'

As they lumbered away from Lycan Point, Justin struggled to contain his panic.

He knew he was the one who'd insisted he and Riley dance in the fundraiser exhibition and he still thought it was a terrific idea. Except for one very, very significant factor:

If Kyle the Skee-Ball Superstar was attending the event, that meant the Beasts would go too. And *that* meant Justin would either have to invent a new dance called the Invisible Cha-Cha . . . or deal with whatever humiliating consequences he'd be sure to face when his teammates saw him on the dance floor.

Thanks to Kyle and his over-competitive skee-ball aspirations, Justin had suddenly gone from feeling like a clever, supportive boyfriend to feeling like a cha-cha-*chump!*

Usually Daniel enjoyed himself during after-school band rehearsals – but today he felt uneasy.

Earlier, he'd overheard Kyle telling the other football players that he'd decided to call off the captain's practice for the day.

Strange, Daniel had thought at the time. *What could be so important that* Kyle *would call off practice?*

Now on stage, Daniel couldn't help but wonder where the Beasts were at this very moment. Unfortunately, he had a pretty good idea.

Be careful up there, Justin, he thought, hoping there was some truth to those kooky myths that twins could communicate telepathically.

Another reason he was having trouble concentrating on the music was the fact that Debi had come along to watch rehearsal. As she danced and clapped along with the songs, her bracelet worked its nasty magic, clogging up his head so badly he could barely hear his bandmates playing.

When they finished, Debi clapped so enthusiastically Daniel had to duck backstage and blow his nose before he unleashed a sneeze louder than their last song. When he returned, Otto was showing Riley sheet music for his and Nathan's latest composition.

'I love it!' Riley said, passing the page over to Daniel. 'The lyrics are really original. Plus, it's perfect for my vocal range.'

127

Daniel eyed the sheet music, and got about halfway through the first verse before the sharps and flats and treble clefs began to blur before his watering eyes. He let out a loud sloppy, sneeze.

'Ugh,' said Otto, snatching the page back. 'Way to get your slimy boogers all over my masterpiece.'

'Sorry,' said Daniel. 'But the song's great. Let's work on it now.'

He'd just arranged his fingers on the strings when the auditorium door opened and Emma came rushing in. Her streaky hair was a wild mess and her cheeks were pink.

'Hi,' she said breathlessly. 'I was wondering if you'd mind if I sat in and listened.'

'Sure,' said Riley. 'Grab a seat.'

Otto spun one of his drumsticks and sighed. 'Great. Now we've got a fan base.'

'What's wrong with a fan base?' asked Debi.

'Fans are for the mainstream,' Otto groaned.

Emma dropped into a seat in the front row. Daniel found himself staring at her hands as they wrestled her windblown hair into a pony tail. Had her fingernails been that long and jagged the other day? He blinked, and looked again, only to see that her nails were a normal length.

When he felt a tap on his shoulder he didn't have to turn to see who it was – the fierce itching in his nose told him exactly whose Silver Doom-sporting hand was doing the tapping.

Unable to hold back, Daniel sneezed right into his mic: *'HHHAAA-CCC-OOOOHHH!'*

The sneeze screamed through the speakers, creating an explosion of static.

Debi, Riley and Nathan winced, clapping their hands over their ears.

129

But Otto and Emma were grinning their heads off.

'Awesome reverb!' she cried out, just as Otto said:

'Now *that's* a sound we should try to get into our act!'

At that, Daniel turned to share a chuckle with Debi, but found her looking back and forth between him and Emma.

The confusion in Debi's eyes put a nervous knot in his gut.

I've been staring at Emma from the minute she came in.

'Can we get back to rehearsing?' asked Nathan. 'Let's see how the new song sounds.'

'No!' Daniel blurted, a genius idea occurring to him. 'Let's play *Moonlight Girl!*' Unfortunately, with his blocked-up sinuses it came out as 'Mootwight Gull'. Even so, Debi would know she had nothing to be jealous about if he sang the song he'd written especially for her. 'I can never get enough of that song,' he added softly.

That did the trick. Debi blushed and smiled.

Riley, on the other hand, plumped her lip out in a pout. 'I don't have anything to do on *Moonlight Girl*. Daniel sings lead vocals, and I don't even have a tambourine to shake.'

'Sorry, Riley,' said Daniel. 'Maybe you can dance in the background.'

The words were out before he realised his mistake; visions of Justin cha-cha-ing around the living room flashed in his brain.

Riley's face paled – she did not want the rest of the band to know about her lessons.

'Uh, I mean . . .' Daniel stammered '. . . did I say "dance"? I meant . . . you can *enhance* the background by harmonising with Otto on the chorus.'

'Good,' huffed Nathan. 'Because fans are one

thing, but we *won't* have back-up dancers.'

They played the song. When it was over, Debi applauded, but Emma stuck her fingers in her mouth and let out a long appreciative whistle.

'You're whistling for that?' Otto grumbled. 'It sounded like Daniel was singing with a clothes peg on his nose.'

'I thought it sounded great,' said Emma, her eyes meeting Daniel's directly. 'I have a soft spot for anything that has to do with moonlight.'

Is this 'Emma Flirting With Daniel — The Sequel'?
Or does she really have a thing for the moon?

He almost jumped out of his skin when the alarm on Riley's watch bleated.

'I almost forgot,' she exclaimed. 'I've got to be . . . *somewhere*. Hope you guys don't mind packing up without me.'

She didn't wait around for their response before hurrying through the split in the curtains

at the back of the stage. Daniel heard a crash –
classic Riley.

As the auditorium fell silent, he sidled up
closer to where Debi was still sitting on his
amplifier – just in case Emma needed a visual
reminder he was part of a very happy couple.

'OK, guys,' he said, 'let's get our gear packed up.'

Nathan and Otto went about removing the
equipment from the stage.

'Thanks for the mini concert,' said Emma,
standing and giving them a friendly wave. 'Maybe
I'll come back next time you rehearse.'

'Um . . .' said Nathan, at the same time that
Otto said, 'That'd be great.'

'Bye, Debi,' said Emma.

'Bye.'

'Bye, Daniel.'

Daniel grunted and kept his focus on getting
his guitar into its case. No easy trick since his

sudden fear that Emma had a crush on him had caused claws to sprout from three of the fingers on his right hand.

'She seems to really dig your music,' Debi commented, in a casual way.

Again, Daniel just grunted and focused on putting away his guitar and not wolfing out. How did he convince his girlfriend that he didn't like another girl? He *didn't* like her . . . but coming clean about the other secret in his life was just not an option.

Daniel sighed. Life had been a lot easier back when he and Justin had thought girls were gross and annoying.

///   ///   ///

Mr Morgan's SUV was waiting for them out front. Daniel had successfully positioned himself on Debi's right for the walk from the auditorium to the parking lot, but when she jumped into the backseat on the passenger's side, he knew he was in trouble. He'd have to get in behind Mr Morgan and this would put him a little too close to the Silver Doom. If only he had some sort of buffer.

Nothing like a big, bulky guitar case to block the power of a tiny silver bracelet.

Daniel opened the car door and stuffed his guitar into the backseat between him and Debi.

'There's plenty of room in the hatchback,' Mr Morgan pointed out, frowning at Daniel in the rearview mirror.

'Oh, well, uh, thanks, Mr Morgan, but I prefer to keep my guitar close at hand.'

Mr Morgan clicked his tongue. 'Let me guess . . . it's a rock-star thing?'

As Mr Morgan pulled out of the parking lot, Daniel tried to think of a topic that would

135

interest Debi's dad, but the only thing that came to mind was the town's 'big dog' problem.

When Mr Morgan hit the indicator to take a right turn on to Main Street the clicking noise was the only sound in the awkwardly conversation-less car.

Finally, Debi came to his rescue . . . sort of.

'So, Daniel Packer,' she said, a teasing lilt in her tone. 'Am I ever gonna get this "terrific birthday present" you have for me?'

Mr Morgan's eyes shot to the rearview mirror again, and he narrowed them at Daniel. 'In my day, son, it was considered impolite to keep a young lady waiting.'

Daniel's scalp tingled and his ears felt as though they were on the verge of stretching into wolfish points.

'I keep meaning to get it to you,' Daniel

explained, 'but there have been some . . . obstacles.'

"'*Obstacles*'?' Mr Morgan said. 'What kind of obstacles could keep a guy from remembering to give his girlfriend a present?' His eyes flashed in the mirror, sending a chill up Daniel's spine. 'Unless, maybe it has something to do with all the "big dog" sightings.'

'Dad!' Debi rolled her eyes. 'What could that *possibly* have to do with anything?'

'Well, you never know,' said Mr Morgan. 'Maybe Daniel's been too preoccupied with this . . . *problem* to remember to give you your gift.'

'Everyone's concerned, Dad,' Debi pointed out. 'Especially because of the Jackson Caulfield movie. But why would Daniel be any more preoccupied than anyone else?'

Daniel's wolf ears picked up Mr Morgan's mumble:

'Good question.' Then he chuckled. 'Maybe the big dog ate your birthday present.'

Debi giggled. 'Dad, that's what you say when you forget your *homework*, not a birthday gift!'

Daniel squirmed. He was just wondering if a ride-long sneezing fit might have been better after all, when suddenly Mr Morgan pulled over to the kerb and brought the car to an abrupt halt in front of the community centre.

Weird. We're still a half mile from our street.

Mr Morgan turned around in the driver's seat to smile at them. 'Hope you don't mind, Daniel,' he said cheerfully. 'Debi's mom asked me to stop off and have Debi's birthday bracelet polished. She thought it was looking a tad tarnished.'

'Really?' said Debi. 'It looks fine to me.'

'Hmm,' said Mr Morgan. 'I have an idea. Let's get Daniel's opinion on whether the bracelet could use a cleaning.' He nodded to Debi.

'Show it to him, honey . . . Up close.'

Daniel's fur-sprouting hand was on the door handle in a flash and his feet were on the pavement before Debi even had a chance to push back the cuff of her blouse.

'I'd love to help,' he said, tugging his clunky guitar case out of the back seat. 'But I really don't know anything about jewellery.'

'OK,' said Debi, sounding disappointed. 'I guess I'll see you in school tomorrow.'

'Can't wait.' Daniel closed the door and waved before hurrying around the corner and out of sight of the car.

I guess I'll go hang out at the community centre and catch a ride home with Mr Carter, when he picks up Riley and Justin.

If nothing else, the wait would give him some time to think . . . about what in the world he could buy to replace the cruddy seashell necklace present, and prove he wasn't a cruddy boyfriend. And also about how to keep Mr Morgan from finding out he was a werewolf!

Chapter Eight

'So I need Maths, History and English,' Justin said, removing the textbooks from his locker.

But he was removing them with *flourishes*. Every time he pulled a book out, he flicked a hand, thrust a hip or dipped into a plié. He knew the added dance moves were slowing things down – a *lot* – but the rhythm was in him, and he couldn't fight it.

'Do you really need to choreograph this process, bro?' Daniel sighed, leaning against the next locker. 'Can't you just put the books in the backpack and quit acting like a contestant on *Dancing With the Stars*?'

Justin closed the locker and spun a perfect pirouette right there in the hallway. 'Can I make a confession?' he said as he and Daniel started off down the hall.

Daniel laughed. 'As long as it doesn't include another one of those spinny-things.'

Justin grinned. 'The word is "pirouette". But if you ever tell anyone I know that term, I'll de-brother you.'

'Don't worry – I'm pretty sure I don't want anyone knowing I have an identical twin who knows that kind of stuff.'

'*Know it?* I'm actually starting to *like* it,' Justin admitted. 'It's been great for my coordination.'

'You've always been coordinated,' Daniel pointed out.

'Not *this* coordinated. Football is all about

power and agility, where dancing is about control and grace. Could you imagine if I could put it all together? I'd be unstoppable.'

'Somehow, I don't think a tutu would go with your football uniform.'

Justin gave him an elbow to the ribs. 'OK, enough about me and my twinkletoes. What is going on with *you*? Last night you were sulking more than usual – which is saying something!'

Daniel looked pointedly at the crowd of passing students. 'Not exactly *appropriate* hallway conversation,' he whispered.

'Daniel,' said Justin, shaking his head, 'do I have to remind you what happened the last time you bottled up a secret?' He threw an arm around his brother's shoulder. 'Whatever's on your mind now can't be anywhere near as "complicated" as finding out you're a . . . you know.'

'You would think,' Daniel muttered. 'But,

seriously, a mouthful of fangs was a lot easier to deal with than disappointing my girlfriend.'

Now they'd come to a place at the end of the hallway where no one was around to hear them. 'Just tell me what the problem is,' Justin prodded.

Daniel opened his mouth and a hurricane of words came out: 'I should never have bragged to Debi about what an "awesome" gift I got her, because that poky little string of seashells is pretty much the suckiest gift ever – so now I have to come up with something awesome instead, and I am seriously out of ideas. And *then* there's this issue with Emma, because she's kind of friendly when she talks to me – although maybe I only *think* she's being friendly. I keep staring, trying to get a better read on her, and Debi keeps catching me staring – and now I have a feeling that, maybe, Debi thinks I'm *interested* in Emma. Plus I have a feeling that Emma might be behind all this "big dog" stuff.'

Daniel was practically blue in the face when he finished. Justin gave his brother a moment to catch his breath.

'What you need to do,' said Justin, 'is quit worrying about Emma and come up with a great gift.'

'OK . . . but what?'

Justin thought for a moment. The more he thought, the more his feet began to tap. Soon he was performing a bouncy little box-step. A look from Daniel made him stop. Boy, he'd be glad when this dance exhibition was over so he could –

'The dance exhibition!'

'Huh?' asked Daniel.

'You can take Debi on a date to the fundraiser, because there's not just skee-ball and a dance exhibition, there's also a major dance *competition*

. . . with judges . . . and Riley found out that one of them is none other than Winifred Peters!'

'The Count Vira lady?'

'Do you know any *other* Winifred Peters?' Justin clapped his brother on the back. 'Bringing Debi to an event where she can be in the same room as her favourite author has *got* to be the best birthday gift of all time.'

'Yeah!' said Daniel. 'Not only will I get Debi in the same room as Winifred Peters, I'll figure out a way to wrangle an introduction *and* an autograph!' Daniel threw Justin an exuberant high five. 'Thanks, bro. Awesome idea.'

'You're welcome,' said Justin. 'But all I said was, get her in the same room. I don't know about this autograph stuff. Apparently this lady's not exactly a social butterfly.'

Now that Justin thought about it, it was probably some kind of miracle that the hospital board had gotten Winifred Peters to agree to show up at such a public event.

'Leave Winifred Peters to me,' said Daniel. 'You can help by getting Riley to sneak the book you two got Debi out of her room so I can bring it to the fundraiser for Count Virus –'

'Vir-*a*.'

'– to sign. It's a perfect birthday present.'

The determination in his brother's eyes made Justin think that if anybody could find a way to bring this quirky author out of her shell, it would be Daniel. 'I'll tell Riley,' he said.

'Thanks.' Daniel looked relieved and excited – for about six seconds. Then, a dark look came into his eyes. Daniel's nose twitched.

'Now what?' asked Justin, a sinking feeling in his gut.

Daniel craned his neck and sniffed the air. 'The she-wolf has been here. In Lupine form.'

'Been *where*?' Justin asked grimly. 'Like two miles away, paying the counter clerk at the Meat & Greet?'

Daniel shook his head. 'Like right here at school.' His eyes had begun to narrow in a wolfish way. 'She was in this hallway just a few minutes ago. She's a student . . . And, if she's a student, there's really only one likely candidate for who she could be . . .'

It was obvious – the 'wolf sightings' had started around the time that she had showed up. 'Emma?'

Daniel nodded.

'So what do we do?'

'We track her,' Daniel answered, his teeth lengthening before Justin's eyes.

'Now?'

Daniel nodded. 'C'mon, bro. Let's run!'

'Let's run,' Justin muttered, rolling his eyes.

'Do you have *any* idea how much I hate it when you werewolves say that?'

But Daniel was gone. Justin took a deep breath, and sprinted after him.

Justin wasn't slow. He'd burned rubber on the field with the Beasts plenty of times, but that was nothing compared to trying to keep up with his brother now. Daniel was wolfed-out and racing around Lycan Point so fast it was all Justin could do to keep him in his sights.

He was relieved when his werewolf brother finally came to a stop at the edge of a clearing.

Wheezing, leg-muscles screaming, Justin flopped down on a fallen log to watch wolf-Daniel press his sweaty muzzle to the dirt.

'What are you going to do if you find her?'

'*When* I find her,' Daniel corrected, scampering to the middle of the clearing. 'I'm going to inform her – politely – that there is a werewolf community here in Pine Wood that would appreciate it if she'd quit running around, risking our secret.'

'And if she doesn't have a "polite" response?'

Daniel didn't answer because something had caught his eye. Justin watched as his twin sprung up to his full wolf height, his pointy ears pressed back, his whiskers quivering.

'There!' he growled, pointing a claw.

Even in the growing darkness it was impossible to miss the flash of brown and white fur, moving through the trees. But the weird thing was that this time, the flash wasn't moving *away* from them.

It was moving *towards* them!

Justin felt a stab of fear. 'Bro, is this one of

those times you're going to say *"Let's run"*, but this time you mean run *away?'*

But Daniel had put his paw up to silence his twin. The brown and white figure continued to move closer.

She's surrendering! Justin gulped. *Either that or she's ready to brawl!*

Justin's heart thudded when, at last, the she-wolf stepped into the clearing. To his surprise, she did not carry herself like Daniel and the Beasts did – upright, on two legs. This creature – with her sleek coat, muscular form and stunning Lupine face – walked on all fours, like a true wolf.

Her eyes were trained on Daniel; his eyes were locked on hers. She stalked to the middle of the clearing until they were separated by about ten yards. Immediately, Daniel sank down so that he, too, was on all fours. Justin wasn't sure if this was to show that he meant no harm, or so that he could better defend himself.

Is this a showdown? A fight to the death?

Or was this how Lupines say, 'Wanna play? Let's be friends!'

Now Daniel tilted his head, eyeing her as they began to circle each other slowly. With his human limbs, Daniel did not move as gracefully as the she-wolf, but they walked in perfect time, completely aware of the other's space – keeping a safe distance, but sharing a rhythm. Justin couldn't help the crazy thought that he was watching a werewolf waltz!

Maybe these two should enter the dance contest!

Then, suddenly, the she-wolf laughed!

At least, Justin *thought* it was a laugh. The sound was a cross between a growl and a snarl. And then she shook her head and spoke:

'Wow, Daniel. It took you long enough!'

Daniel's ears flattened back in surprise. 'What are you talking about?'

The next thing Justin knew she was standing on her hind legs. Her ears grew smaller and her pert snout sank back into her face; her fur seemed to shimmer as it retreated into her skin and her front legs became arms.

It *was* Emma!

'Took you long enough to find me,' she said in her normal human voice.

Justin and Daniel just gaped at her until she rolled her eyes.

'You *have* been looking for me, haven't you?'

'Yes. Well, no.' Daniel took a moment to de-wolf. 'At first the town was just keeping watch for a big dog.'

'And then our dad told us about she-wolves,' said Justin, moving into the clearing. 'So we were looking for one of those. But we were never completely sure it was you.'

Again, Emma laughed, although Justin had to admit, her laughing as a girl was a much nicer sound than as a wolf.

'You weren't *sure*?' She sighed. 'Daniel, I gave you so many hints!'

'Hints?'

'Yes, hints. At the football field, and at your band practice. Didn't you pick up on them?'

Justin was aware that his brother had suddenly gone red in the face.

'Uh, well . . . kind of . . .' Daniel stammered. 'But I thought . . .'

Justin grinned. 'He thought you were flirting with him,' he explained to Emma. 'And as much as I'd love to hang around and hear your reaction to *that*, I've gotta split. Riley and I have . . . an appointment.'

Emma shot him a teasing look. 'And by

154

appointment you mean dance class, right?'

'So it *was* you I saw outside the window!'

'Who else?' Emma grinned. 'You do a mean cha-cha-cha, Justin Packer!'

Justin laughed. 'OK, well, I'm outta here. I'll just leave you two Lupines to, er . . . howl at the moon?'

'How about, *discuss why she's been putting the entire wolf community at risk?*' Daniel said sternly.

Emma dipped her head, embarrassed. 'Yeah . . . sorry about that.'

'Work it out, cubs,' Justin advised. 'I've got some shimmying to do.'

As he made his way back through the dark forest, Justin realised he wasn't in the least bit afraid of being up at Lycan Point at night, all alone. He was still scared of one thing, though – something a lot more terrifying than a wild mutt, a werewolf, or even a wild, free-thinking she-wolf.

The humiliation when the Beasts saw him dance at the fundraiser tomorrow.

What could be scarier than that?

///   \\\   ///

Daniel and Emma had come out of the woods and were sitting on a rock on the edge of Lycan Point. Below them, the town of Pine Wood looked warm and snug. Windows glowed golden and streetlamps sparked to life.

Nothing to worry about tonight, Pine-Woodians, Daniel thought with a chuckle. *The big bad dog is nothing but a friendly she-wolf.*

'So,' said Emma, 'let me repeat that I absolutely wasn't flirting with you. I was just dropping subtle clues that you and I had a lot in common.' She gave him a playful elbow to the ribs. 'I know you're with Debi – who's great, by the way.'

Daniel relaxed. 'So why didn't you just tell me you were a she-wolf?'

'Hmm, let's see.' Emma scratched her chin in pretend thought. 'New girl walks up to one of the coolest guys in school and says, "Hi, I am an extremely rare creature known as a she-wolf, and my presence here is going to upset the entire balance of your secret wolf world. Wanna study for algebra together?"'

Daniel laughed. Mainly at her 'coolest guys in school' comment. 'So, instead, you run around town, making people twitchy?'

Emma sighed. 'I stayed indoors for so long,' she said, 'but it's hard to keep yourself locked up when you have so much power and energy. Eventually, my parents started letting me out to run – Lycan Point is great for that.'

Daniel blinked. 'They trusted you?'

'Completely,' said Emma. 'She-wolves have

great control. But my dad still wanted me to hold off announcing myself until he could make his own proper introduction to the wolf community. My parents moved us to Pine Wood because they heard what a large wolf community you had here. We were even hoping there'd be at least one other teenage she-wolf in your pack for me to hang out with.' She turned a hopeful expression to Daniel.

Daniel hated to disappoint her, but he shook his head. 'You're the first and only.'

Emma shrugged. 'Oh, well. So much for all those giggly she-wolf sleepovers I was planning.'

'As far as I know,' said Daniel, 'there have never been any lady Lupines anywhere around here. But Debi and Riley are really cool girls, and they both already like you.' He frowned. 'Well, at least Debi *did* like you, but I think she thought *I* liked you. Now maybe she doesn't like either of us.'

'You're going to have to run that one by me again.'

Daniel explained how Debi had caught him staring at Emma and that he was afraid she had misread his interest.

'I don't think that'll be a problem,' Emma said. 'Now that you know the truth, you won't have to stare any more.'

That was good news to Daniel. But he was still curious about one thing.

'If you weren't interested in me, what was with the dreamy-eyes during band rehearsal?'

'Well, you're not the only guy in In Sheep's Clothing.'

Daniel's eyes flew open. This was huge . . . in a good way! 'Who were you looking at?' he prodded. 'Nathan or Otto?'

Emma blushed deeply. 'Not telling.'

'You were OK with telling me you're one of

the rarest mythological creatures ever to roam the earth, but you *won't* tell me which one of my band mates you're crushing on?'

She nodded.

'C'mon!' Daniel couldn't help laughing.

'Nope.' Emma gave him a mock growl.

Daniel was willing to drop it . . . for now, anyway. 'So what's it like?' he asked softly. 'Turning full wolf when you're so young, and having to handle all the power so early.'

'It's challenging,' Emma admitted in a serious tone. 'I mean, c'mon. Being a fully mature werewolf before you're even old enough to drive is not without its complications. The good part is how in tune with nature I am when I'm in wolf form. My dad explained that although male werewolves have enhanced senses, they're nothing compared to those of a she-wolf. It's such a feeling of power.' She shrugged again.

'I guess that's the trade-off. I have no choice but to tough it out through the loneliness.'

Daniel reached over and nudged her arm. 'You won't be lonely in Pine Wood. I promise.'

'Of course not,' she said, her eyes sparkling now. 'How could I be when I've got half the football team putting on a circus every time I walk in a room?' She cocked an eyebrow. 'That brings up an interesting point.'

'More interesting than whether you like Nathan or Otto?' Daniel asked, grinning.

'Way more interesting.' She gave him a long look. 'Before you suspected I was a she-wolf, you should have been operating on pure instinct. The minute we met that first day, you should have started acting like a total show-off.'

Daniel nodded. 'I've been wondering why I've never once felt the urge to stand on my head, or leap over the school building or anything like that when you're around. Uh, no offence,' he added quickly.

'None taken.'

Daniel frowned, puzzling it out. 'Maybe it has to do with my nose being stuffed up. I've only been around you when Debi's nearby, and when Debi's nearby, I can hardly breathe.'

'Wow.' Emma smiled dreamily. 'That's so romantic.'

'No, I don't mean it that way. I mean, I *am* nuts about her. But she just got this silver bracelet for her birthday, and it gets my nose so stuffed up it must swamp all my other senses!' He grinned.

'To be honest,' said Emma, 'I'm glad you're immune. I've got enough guys turning cartwheels for me. It's nice to have one male friend who can keep it together in my presence.'

'What about Nathan?' Daniel teased. 'Bet you wouldn't mind having him do a few somersaults on your behalf. Or maybe it's Otto who you'd like to see strut his stuff?'

Emma glared at him, but he could see the smile behind it. 'I'll make you a deal. You stop pestering me about your bandmates, and not only will I quit running around Pine Wood in wolf-form, I'll tell you how to battle a certain bracelet that's been making your life miserable.'

'You can do that?' Daniel sat up straight. *This could be the best news since they offered fifty per cent off at the Meat & Greet.*

'Have you ever seen *me* so much as sniffle when Debi's around?'

She had a point. 'You've got a deal. Spill it!'

'Kumquat!'

'What-quat?'

Emma chuckled. 'Kumquat juice has been saving werewolves from silver for centuries. It's like an antidote. All you have to do is squeeze the juice, add a little sugar, mix with water and *voila* – instant immunity.'

'That's amazing.' Daniel could have wept with relief. He'd hate to have to choose between the girl he liked and the ability to breathe.

'I'd be happy to give you a few bottles,' said Emma, as they hopped off the rock and headed for her house.

I've got a brother, Daniel thought to himself. *But now that Emma's here, I'm going to know what it feels like to have a sister, too.*

Chapter Nine

When Daniel and Emma reached the Sharpes' front door, Emma paused.

'Maybe you should wait out here,' she said. 'We're still unpacking and the place is a mess. My mom will flip out if the first person I invited over sees our house in this condition.'

Daniel laughed. 'No problem. My mom's a clean freak, too.'

When Emma went inside, Daniel thought about how he had passed by this house a zillion times, but it had never occurred to him that one of the most unique specimens of Lupine life would be living in it one day.

A few minutes later, he heard a car rounding the corner at the end of the street, just as Emma returned with the water.

'Here you go,' she said, handing him some bottles. 'It's already mixed, so all you have to do is carry it around and drink from it like an ordinary water bottle. '

Now Daniel understood. The day of Debi's school tour, Emma had been sipping from a plastic bottle. Yesterday in the auditorium she hadn't gotten close enough to Debi to feel the effects of Silver Doom, so it hadn't mattered that she didn't have a bottle with her.

'You have no idea how much I appreciate this,' said Daniel. 'Thanks. It'll be nice to be able to stand next to my girlfriend without breaking into a sneezing frenzy.' Daniel pulled Emma into a big, brotherly hug, just as the car reached the Sharpe house.

Screeeeeeeaaaaachhhhhh!

Without warning, the driver slammed on the brakes.

'Jeesh, what's *his* problem?' Emma asked.

But Daniel knew *exactly* what the problem was! The car that had come to a squealing halt in the middle of the street was Mr Morgan's!

Debi was in the passenger seat, and she and her father were staring at him, standing on the Sharpes' front porch, with his arms around Emma!

Daniel's girlfriend's eyes met his for only a second, narrowing with confusion before turning away in disbelief.

Daniel was so panicked that he turned on the super-speed, bolting from the porch, across the lawn, and to the car in less than a heartbeat.

Luckily, Debi was still looking away, and didn't see his blurred approach.

167

But Mr Morgan might have. Daniel couldn't worry about that at the moment, though. Right now, seeing Debi so distraught was tearing his heart to pieces.

He knocked on the passenger's side window. 'Debi . . . open up.'

She said nothing – she just turned and looked at him, as if to ask what excuse he was going to offer. Daniel could not even think of a lame one.

I'm such a terrible boyfriend. He had to concentrate with his entire being to keep from turning wolf. Debi rolled the window down halfway.

'It's not what it looks like,' Daniel gushed.

'It *looks like* you were hugging Emma Sharpe,' Debi said, her voice cold.

'OK . . .' Daniel gulped. 'Then it *is* what it looks like. But, honest, I was not hugging her the way I –' He caught himself before the words *I hug you* made it out of his mouth.

'Daniel . . .' said Debi. 'Tell me the truth. What's going on?'

I'm a werewolf, Emma's a she-wolf, and those bottles of kumquat juice she gave me just might be my only hope for ever holding your hand again.

'Uh . . . the reason I was hugging Emma just now is because I was thanking her. For helping me . . . with something.' If he didn't say too much more, he wouldn't even have to lie.

'And what would that be?' Mr Morgan asked curtly.

Mr Morgan was forcing him to say more. *Oh, just an ancient werewolf antidote. You've probably heard of it, being a monster expert and all.*

Then a flash of inspiration hit. 'Debi's birthday present!' he yelped. 'I needed Emma's help with something to make this already unbelievable gift even cooler.'

Debi considered this, her gaze softening just a little. 'That . . . makes sense. Birthday present.'

'*Belated* birthday present,' Mr Morgan corrected.

'So is everything good?' Daniel asked Debi a tad desperately.

Debi didn't look completely convinced, but she didn't look furious, either. 'I guess,' she said. 'And Daniel, I really am touched that you're working so hard to make my present special.'

'Might have been more special if it came *on time*,' Mr Morgan murmured.

'I'm happy to do it for you,' Daniel assured Debi, his knees almost buckling with relief.

'*I'd* be happy if we could be on our way now,' snapped Mr Morgan. 'So please step away from the vehicle . . . Speedy.'

Uh-oh!

Daniel was saved by a beep from Debi's phone.

'It's a text from Mom,' she reported. 'Dinner's almost ready.'

'Well, I guess I'll just get out of your way then,' said Daniel, stepping away from the SUV. 'Nice to see you again, Mr Morgan. Debi, I'll talk to you tomorrow.'

She gave him a smile, but there was still a shadow of doubt in her eyes when she waved goodbye.

Daniel nearly collapsed. He heard Emma on her porch, stifling a giggle.

'I almost blew it that time!' Daniel whispered.

'I think you made a pretty good save,' Emma said. 'But there is one problem. You set the bar even higher for this mysterious birthday gift.'

Daniel brightened. 'Oh, I came up with an awesome idea this afternoon. On Saturday night, my birthday blues will be over!'

'Birthday Blues,' Emma mused. 'That would

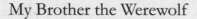
be a great title for a song. You should mention it to Nathan.'

'Ah! So it's Nathan, huh?'

Emma grinned, shaking her head and turning up her palms.

Smiling, Daniel rolled his eyes. 'She-wolves,' he muttered.

'Werewolves,' she hissed back.

Only a handful of Miss Samantha's students showed up for the three o'clock session on Saturday afternoon, Justin and Riley among them.

'I'm glad you two came,' Miss Samantha told them. 'You're really making progress and this last-minute rehearsal will have you looking dynamite tonight!'

Justin spun Riley into an elegant twirl. Inspired

by the fact that she managed to remain on her feet, he spun her back, then swept her into a graceful dip.

'Excellent!' cried Miss Samantha, applauding.

Justin smiled down at Riley. 'We're really getting the hang of this, huh?' he said.

For the next several minutes, they waltzed around the floor with the rest of the couples, while Miss Samantha flitted here and there making corrections and offering praise. 'You're all completely on point today,' she said, smiling. 'But remember, impressing the judges is not enough.'

Her bright smile was suddenly replaced with a look of steely resolve.

'You have to be fabulous out there tonight, people!' Her eyes glinted with determination. 'You've got to be better than your best. You've got to *win*!'

'Wow,' Justin whispered. 'She sounds like Coach Johnston right now. Maybe we should fix them up.'

'Yes, let's!' cried Riley. 'They'd make a cute couple.'

'I was kidding,' said Justin. The last thing he needed was for his football coach to start dating his dance teacher.

I never thought I'd ever have a dance teacher!

'I guess you're right,' said Riley. 'Besides, the only cute couple we should be focusing on right now is –'

'Us?' Justin gave her a big goofy grin.

She giggled, and whacked him gently on the arm. 'You know I'm always focused on us. I was talking about Daniel and Debi; I wish I knew what was up with them.'

Justin considered telling Riley the truth about the she-wolf discovery, and also that Daniel worried his curiosity over Emma may have led Debi to believe he was *into* the new girl. But he knew Riley would be concerned for her friends' relationship; she might even try to do something to fix it. Today, Justin didn't want her concentrating on anything besides dancing. Specifically, dancing with *him*! So instead of going into a detailed explanation of the current Daniel-and-Debi-drama, he simply said, 'They'll work it out. Especially after he gets Winifred Peters' autograph.'

Riley's eyes sparkled. 'I'm just glad Debi invited me to sleep over last night. It gave me a chance to sneak her copy of *Everlasting Night* out of her room.'

It was all Justin could do to keep from kissing her right there on the dance floor! *Is my girlfriend the sweetest girl on the planet or what?*

This heart-swelling thought was interrupted

175

by a very familiar cackle.

'Samantha, shouldn't you be herding these so-called "dancers" out of here?' Miranda sneered. 'I believe the community centre lets this space to a Dog Obedience instructor at this hour. Of course, those of us who *own* our studios never have to worry about that sort of thing.'

'We were just leaving,' Samantha said crisply.

'Good,' Miranda snapped, glancing around the room. 'Because soon, this place will be filled with unruly terriers, misbehaving hounds and hysterical toy poodles.' She gave the couples exiting the floor a look of disdain. 'Though I suspect even *they'll* look more like dancers.'

Justin gritted his teeth as a tittering Miranda sashayed out the door.

Samantha fled to the back of the room, while the dancers made a hasty exit. The teacher flung leotards, tights and dance slippers into her bag.

Justin was all for following the other students out the door, but Riley wasn't budging.

'You want to go talk to her?' he asked, knowing the answer.

'We can't leave without seeing if she's all right.'

'Fine.' Justin sighed. 'Let's meddle.'

They made their way to where Samantha was zipping up her dance bag.

'Is there anything we can do?' Riley asked softly.

Samantha shook her head. 'You're sweet to ask, but I don't think there's any way to get Miranda to stop harassing me.'

'Maybe we can set one of those "misbehaving hounds" on her,' Justin quipped.

Samantha laughed. 'I wouldn't mind seeing Miranda chased down the street by an unruly terrier or two. But that would only solve half the problem.'

'What do you mean?' asked Riley.

'It's the dance contest,' Samantha explained. 'I suppose you've sensed how badly I want my students to win.'

'Yeah,' said Justin. 'We picked up on that.'

'Well, part of the reason is silly. The head judge is the man who taught Miranda and me when we were younger. He always favoured her because she was such a fierce competitor.' Miss Samantha looked at the floor. 'I guess I'm hoping to prove to him that I'm just as qualified as she is.'

Justin totally understood that motivation. Hadn't he gone out of his way to prove to the Beasts he wasn't an inferior athlete?

'There's a more practical reason, too,' Samantha went on. 'The people who run the community centre feel it's not necessary to offer dance classes here when there's a real dance studio right across the street. Since I'm just a pay-

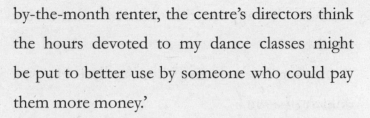

by-the-month renter, the centre's directors think the hours devoted to my dance classes might be put to better use by someone who could pay them more money.'

'Doesn't really have much of a "community" ring to it, does it?' Riley pointed out.

'No, but I can't say I blame them,' sighed Miss Samantha, slinging her dance bag over her shoulder. 'I can't expect them to keep losing money for my sake.'

Justin hated to admit it but she had a point.

'*Does* Miranda have a stronger reputation?' Riley asked.

Samantha nodded. 'But in all modesty, it has more to do with her shouting louder, than her teaching ability. That's why I'm so keen to have my students win this competition. When people see what my dancers can do, they might leave Miranda and study with me.' She frowned,

179

blushing. 'I suppose that sounds unbelievably cut-throat?'

'A little,' said Justin. 'But it's not like she doesn't deserve it.'

By now, the dogs and their owners had begun to arrive, which was their cue to leave. The minute Justin and Riley set foot outside the door, he wished they too had opted for the rear exit. Sauntering down Main Street were Kyle and the Beasts.

They stopped when they saw Justin.

'Dude,' cried Ed. 'What are you doin' here?'

'What do you think he's doin'?' Caleb said. 'He's goin' to Obedience School.'

The Beasts howled with laughter.

'Seriously,' said Chris. 'Please tell me you didn't just come out of that dorky three o'clock ballroom dance class.'

Instantly, Justin's mind began to whirl,

looking for a believable excuse.

Then Riley came to his rescue.

'Actually, we just came by to post a flyer for my Guatemalan book drive on the bulletin board.' She smiled sweetly at Chris. 'But I'm curious, Christopher . . . how do *you* know there's a three o'clock dance class?'

Kyle swung his head around to frown at Chris. 'Yeah. How *do* you know?'

Chris stuffed his hands in his pockets and stared at the sidewalk. 'My mom made me take a couple of classes last summer,' he confessed, 'so I could waltz with my little sister at our grandparents' anniversary party.'

Caleb snorted. 'I would have paid big money to have seen that.'

'It wasn't pretty,' Chris admitted. 'I accidentally stepped on my sister's foot.'

'That's what happens when you try to teach

a football player to dance!' Kyle chuckled. He nodded to Justin. 'We'll see you tonight at the fundraiser. I expect you to be cheering me on in the skee-ball contest, bro.'

'Wouldn't miss it for the world,' Justin assured him.

When the Beasts had swaggered off, Justin took Riley's hand. 'Thanks,' he said. 'But I'm wondering why we bothered – they're going to know all about it tonight anyway.'

'I don't know,' said Riley, giving him an adorable shrug. 'I guess I just wanted you to have a few more hours of being able to hold your head up without being ashamed.'

'Hey,' said Justin, giving her hand a squeeze. 'I am *never* ashamed to be doing anything with you! Including dancing. No guy could ever be prouder than I am when I'm around you, Riley Carter.'

Riley's mouth fell open in a dainty little O of

surprise. 'Wow,' she whispered. 'That's the most romantic thing I've ever heard.'

'Yeah, well . . .' Justin leaned in and kissed her on the cheek, 'it's not romantic . . . it's true.'

'You know,' said Riley as they headed off down the street hand-in-hand. 'I'm glad I'm learning grace and coordination, but I have to say, there's one major fall I'm awfully glad I took.'

'Which one was that?' Justin asked.

She smiled. 'The one when I fell for you!'

'And you call *me* cheesy,' he joked.

/// \\\ ///

When Justin arrived home, he tangoed straight into the kitchen for a glass of milk and a piece of warm apple pie. He found his twin sitting down, gripping a plastic water bottle. Two more just like it stood on the tabletop.

Justin cut himself a big slice of pie. He motioned to the water bottles. 'Thirsty?'

'Something like that,' Daniel muttered, bringing the bottle to his lips.

'Important to stay hydrated.' Justin broke off a flaky piece of pie crust and popped it into his mouth. 'By the way, Riley swiped the book from Debi's room. I left it on the hall table for you.'

'Hmm.' Daniel took a sip from the bottle, nearly gagged, then gulped it down. 'Thanks.'

'No problem. Speaking of Riley, we had a great rehearsal, but I'm still kind of freaked out about performing tonight in front of the Beasts.'

'Mmmm hmmmm,' said Daniel, throwing back another big swallow of water, then cringing. 'Uhhhccckkk.' Daniel polished off the first bottle, then opened the second. He gritted his teeth for a moment before drinking down the entire contents in one long chug. He gasped and coughed, grimacing as he answered: 'They might not come to watch. I mean, I don't see those guys *wanting* to see fancy dancing.'

'I guess,' said Justin, stuffing another heaped forkful into his mouth. Then he had an idea. 'What if you pretended to be me tonight? Not for the dance exhibition – I'd never do that to Riley – but maybe you can be me and lure the Beasts away from the fundraiser. Maybe tell them you saw the big dog skulking around school. It might be fun – we haven't done a switch in, like, two weeks, right?' He took a gulp of milk, then slumped in his chair. 'No, that won't work. Emma's been keeping a low profile. The whole town's sure the dog is gone! In fact, on my way

185

home from class, I saw the first batch of film production trucks rolling into town.'

'I saw them, too,' Daniel muttered, sipping grimly from the third bottle.

'Besides, I can't ask you to miss the fundraiser. You've got that whole birthday present thing happening, and that's important to you. Debi is important to you.'

Important to you . . .

Justin slapped his palms on the table. 'And Riley is important to me! Way more important than what the Beasts think. I'm going to dance, and I don't care who sees.'

Now that Justin had his priorities in order, he felt exhilarated. He sprung up from his seat, tiptoed through a quick little waltz move, then headed for the kitchen doorway.

When he got there, he stopped dead, turned back and frowned at his twin.

'Daniel?'

'Hm?'

'*What* in the world are you *drinking*?!'

Chapter Ten

The fundraiser would start in an hour. Daniel figured the VIP guests – AKA Winifred Peters – would arrive early, so he'd been standing outside the hospital for three hours, hoping to catch her on her way in. So far, he'd witnessed the arrival of the caterers, the orchestra and the mayor.

But no sign of the author.

He was holding Debi's copy of *Everlasting Night*, with the author photo on the back of the dust jacket. It showed a pleasant-looking woman about his mom's age, with big, amber eyes and light brown hair streaked with pale blonde.

His plan was to approach Winifred and explain the whole dismal story of the seashell necklace and his desperate need to give the world's most amazing girl the world's most amazing gift.

'*That's where you come in, Ms Peters,*' he'd say. '*If you'll just meet my girlfriend later this evening, and sign this book for her, it will be the best birthday present ever.*'

He was hoping that a person who made her living writing about true love would understand how important this gesture was.

He needed her to say yes. So he hid behind a tree and waited. He was so focused on the hospital entrance that he never even heard the security guard sidle up beside him.

'Something I can help you with, kid?'

Daniel jumped. *So much for wolf hearing.* 'N-n-no thanks. I'm good.'

The guard, who towered over Daniel, folded

189

his muscular arms and frowned. 'Well, would you mind telling me why you're lurking around here?'

'I can explain,' Daniel began. 'Let me explain . . .' he mumbled, as he realised that an explanation probably wasn't going to come to him. He got the feeling that this big dude, with his bushy beard and gruff manner, had probably never read a romance novel in his life, and would not care how 'awesome' it would be to get this writer's autograph for your girlfriend.

'I'm waiting . . .' said the guard.

Daniel had no choice but to tell the truth. 'I'm not planning to do anything bad.'

'Glad to hear it.'

'I'm here on a mission of the heart.'

The guard frowned. 'You're waiting to see a cardiologist?'

Daniel shook his head. 'No, a romance writer. I really want to get her to sign this book . . .'

Daniel held it up. 'For my girlfriend's birthday. But this writer is super private, so the only way I can get her to autograph the book is to surprise her here and, well . . . I'm prepared to beg if I have to.'

Daniel was sure the big guy would burst out laughing, but instead he looked away and gave what sounded like a sniffle. 'That's beautiful, kid. I had my first love when I was about your age, so believe me, I know what you're going through.' He wiped his eye with the back of his hand. 'You can wait here all night if you want.'

Daniel stared at the guard, stunned. 'Thanks.'

The guard nodded and smiled. But then his look turned gruff again. 'But you can't take that water in.' He grabbed the bottle from Daniel and threw it in the nearest trash can.

'Nooooo!' he said, but it was too late, the kumquat juice had gone. Daniel just had to hope that the litre and a half he had drunk earlier would be enough to thwart the Silver Doom.

And then his ears pricked up at a noise:

Putt-rrr-vrroommm-putt-rrr-vrrooommm-putt-errrrrr . . .

It took a moment to identify the sound as a small motor going at full throttle. He whirled to see a pink Vespa scooter zipping up the hospital driveway. Could *this* be the world-famous writer? He'd been expecting a stretch limo, but if Winifred Peters was as quirky as everyone said, maybe this actually made more sense.

The driver puttered up to the kerb and cut the motor.

Daniel held his breath as she removed her helmet . . . revealing a cascade of glossy brown hair with gleaming white streaks. Daniel's eyes shot down to the book jacket. The lady on the Vespa looked a little older than she did in the photo but there was no question in his mind that this was the one and only Winifred Peters.

He sprang out from behind the tree. 'Ms Peters!' he called. 'May I talk to you for a second?'

Winifred Peters let out a little squeal of surprise. In one lightning-fast movement, she hopped off the Vespa and dashed into the hospital, her red purse flying behind her.

Daniel stopped in his tracks, his heart sinking. No wonder she'd run . . . she was a recluse, after all, and probably wasn't used to being shouted at by some kid, running towards her waving a book in the air.

He couldn't follow her – not even that big old softie of a guard would let him do that. And once the fundraiser began, he'd never get close enough to plead his case. Debi would not get her personal introduction, or her autographed book. And Daniel would have to break down and tell her the truth: he'd bought her a lousy gift, and even after he'd come up with a sure-fire way to make up for it, he'd failed.

He approached the glass doors of the hospital, thinking perhaps Winifred Peters would still be in the lobby. Maybe he could calmly explain why he'd been screaming her name.

But when he pressed his face to the glass, the lobby was empty.

Winifred Peters, AKA Count Vira, was gone.

Just like his last shred of hope.

※ ※ ※

As long as Justin didn't think about the teasing he'd have to endure from the Beasts, he was almost able to enjoy himself.

Almost.

He was way too nervous to have actual fun.

194

And it wasn't just the Beasts, he was anxious about the dancing itself. Sure, they'd looked great at rehearsal this afternoon, but what if he got confused and two-stepped when he was supposed to cha-cha? Riley would be mortified.

Keep it together! Focus on the party.

The place looked great for a hospital cafeteria. It had been strung with miles of colourful streamers and there were balloon bouquets and arches all around the enormous room. The orchestra sounded terrific as the dancers swirled through their warm-up.

Justin had arrived at the charity event with his team, who left him no choice but to head for the skee-ball section. Kyle was so distracted by his competitiveness, he hadn't remarked on the fact that Justin had turned up in a white shirt and slacks, when the rest of them were in their usual jeans and jackets. The quarterback rolled the balls

195

expertly up the aisle, where they bounced into the air and landed – bullseye – directly into the furthest hole for 100 points. The quarterback hadn't been lying about his talents, Justin realised. Kyle was a skee-ball whizz!

Justin and Riley were planning to meet at seven o'clock sharp, right before the exhibition was scheduled to begin.

'I am the master!' cried Kyle, fist-pumping for joy as he earned another skee-ball high score.

'Save some for the contest,' Justin advised.

'Good point, Packer,' said Kyle. 'Don't want to waste my strength. Let's see what they've got for grub around here.'

As the Beasts made their way boisterously across the room to the refreshment table, Justin saw many familiar faces. It seemed the community-minded people of Pine Wood had come out in droves to support the children's hospital. They mingled happily, drinking punch and tasting *hors d'oeuvres*, as they chatted about the movie production that had arrived in town that afternoon.

One of the familiar faces Justin spotted on his way to the food table was Debi's. She was standing with her parents, making polite conversation with Mayor Graham. Justin caught her eye and waved, but she barely smiled. He knew why of course . . . Daniel was nowhere to be seen.

'Bro, if you can hear me,' Justin said in the softest of whispers, 'you'd better get here quick. Your girlfriend does not look happy.'

As they approached the refreshment table, Justin found himself praying there would be nothing but raw vegetables and dainty pastries – anything the Beasts would find unappealing enough to send them looking elsewhere for 'grub'.

But there must have been a werewolf or two on the hospital's event planning committee because in addition to the veggies and sweets, there was plenty of super-rare roast beef, baby back ribs and other meaty selections.

While his teammates feasted, Justin watched the couples gliding around the dance floor. He recognised many of them from Samantha's class. The others, he assumed, were Miranda's students. He hated to admit it, but they were pretty good. He glanced around and saw Samantha, watching intently as the dancers practised their steps.

Poor Samantha. She looks almost as nervous as I feel.

A sour-faced man in a white tuxedo and hair like Albert Einstein was wandering through the couples, sizing up the dancers with a cold glare. Based on their performances now, he would select four couples to compete later on in the

198

evening. This man was the head judge *and* Miss Samantha's old dance teacher – Louis Gutterson! No wonder Samantha was so nervous. This guy was a big deal in the world of dance.

At the edge of the dance floor, Miranda was beaming wickedly. Justin could tell she thought she had this contest in the bag.

'Back to skee-ball, cubs!' Kyle said, wiping a glob of barbecue sauce from his chin.

As Ed, Chris and Caleb fell into line to follow their captain, Justin hung back.

'Problem, Packer?'

'I'm going to wait here for my brother. I haven't seen him yet.'

'He just walked in,' said Chris, pointing across the room. 'And he looks pretty bummed out.'

Justin looked in the direction Chris had indicated. There was Daniel, moping near the bandstand. And Riley, in a pretty pink dress, was with him. She must have just arrived, too.

Wait! If she's here, that must mean . . . Justin checked the wall clock, and his stomach lurched. Five minutes to seven! The dance exhibition was about to begin.

As he started to cross the dance floor a nasal voice boomed through the cafeteria.

'Good evening, ladies and gentlemen.' Louis Gutterson was standing on a small stage, looking scornfully down his nose at the crowd.

'I'm sure you all know who I am . . .' Gutterson continued.

'You're the guy who discovered the Theory of Relativity!' Caleb shouted.

A ripple of laughter rolled through the crowd.

'I am the judge for tonight's dance contest,' the dance troupe director snapped into the microphone. 'The warm-up period for the competitive dancers is now officially over. In order to give

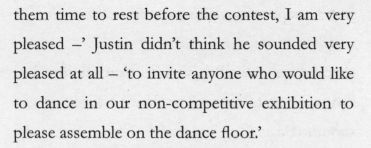

them time to rest before the contest, I am very pleased –' Justin didn't think he sounded very pleased at all – 'to invite anyone who would like to dance in our non-competitive exhibition to please assemble on the dance floor.'

This is it! Daniel's problem would have to wait.

Justin watched as Riley began to make her way on to the dance floor. He knew he should be doing the same thing, but he couldn't make his feet move.

He was frozen, watching Riley stop in the centre of the floor and look around for him.

A very nervous Justin lifted one foot, but instead of moving forwards, his knees buckled and he nearly fell flat on his face! Chris caught him before he hit the floor.

But Justin almost wished he hadn't. Because *now* he understood . . .

So this is what it feels like to wipe out in public, to

topple over yourself and have everyone think you're an uncoordinated klutz.

All those times Riley had tripped, stumbled or fallen down, all those times she'd felt gangly and awkward . . . *this* is what that felt like. It wasn't just embarrassing – it was terrifying. But his girlfriend had been brave enough to do something about it. No way was Justin going to let her down now. So he took a deep breath of his own.

And then he met Riley in the centre of the dance floor.

'Dude,' called Kyle. 'Move! That's for the dancers!'

Justin didn't answer. He was too busy looking into Riley's eyes.

'It's not too late to back out,' she whispered.

'No chance,' Justin whispered back. Justin swept a low and elegant bow, then rose and took her hand.

'Dashing!' she giggled.

He kissed the back of her hand. 'May I have this dance?'

As Justin arranged his hand on Riley's back the way Samantha had taught him, he spied the Beasts out of the corner of his eye. He fully expected them to be rolling on the floor laughing, but they were just staring at him in disbelief.

He was pretty sure it was the first time those guys had ever been speechless.

The orchestra leader counted to four, then the cafeteria was once again filled with music and they began to waltz.

Riley was incredible! The natural turn, the closed changes, the reverse turn — all those fancy moves they'd learned from Samantha were executed to perfection. Before Justin's eyes, Riley had transformed into a graceful princess. She danced as though she'd been born to do it.

As the music rose and swelled, Riley never mistook a single step. In fact, it was *Justin* who nearly broke their rhythm.

But he had a good reason: it was easy to get flustered when you look up to see two very famous people.

Jackson Caulfield and Olivia Abbott.

A second later, Riley saw them, too. Even as she gaped at the dazzling couple, though, she didn't falter.

Jackson gave them his trademark, mega-watt smile. 'Hey, you two are really good at this waltz thing,' he said, as he moved and twirled beside them.

'Thanks,' Justin managed to croak. 'S-so are you.'

Jackson nodded his thanks, and Olivia smiled. In the next beat, they'd gracefully spun away.

'Was that who I think it was?' Justin asked. 'I mean, you're the Jackson Caulfield expert.'

Riley nodded. 'It was totally him. And Olivia Abbott. What are they doing here?'

'The movie . . . *Eternal Sunset* . . . it's shooting here, remember?'

'I know *that*!' said Riley. 'I didn't mean what are they doing here in Pine Wood, I meant what are they doing here at the hospital fundraiser?'

Justin thought back to the poster they'd seen at Miss Miranda's school and grinned. 'I guess they're the "special celebrity guests". As well as Winifred Peters.'

Riley was shaking her head in stunned disbelief. 'It's incredible! Jando, dancing right next to us!'

The song finished and the crowd cheered. Mayor Graham rushed up to the stage and plucked the microphone from its stand. Her strawberry blonde curls bobbed as she nodded around at the dancers.

'You were wonderful, all of you,' she said into the mic. 'Congratulations.'

'Hey, what about the skee-ball contest?' came a wolfish holler from the back of the cafeteria.

'Oh, yes,' said Mayor Graham, flustered. 'I almost forgot. I'd like to announce that the skee-ball contest winner is Pine Wood Junior High football captain, Kyle Hunter!'

The crowd clapped politely, while the Beasts howled and whooped.

'Congratulations, Kyle. You may claim your prize at the bandstand.' Mayor Graham flashed a beaming smile at the party-goers. 'And now, it is my very, very great pleasure to introduce to you our special celebrity guests!' She swept her arm towards the judges' platform. 'She is not only one of the best-selling authors in the country, she is also a thoroughly delightful person. Ladies and gentlemen, Ms Winifred Peters.'

Winifred, who was seated on a folding chair on the judges' platform, looked incredibly embarrassed. She lifted the water bottle she'd been drinking from in a salute, but kept her eyes downcast.

'But we have two more surprise stars here today, too,' Mayor Graham said. 'I am truly honoured to introduce to you two of the most beloved young stars in Hollywood . . . Olivia Abbott and Jackson Caulfield.'

A spotlight burst on, casting a brilliant circle around the two young actors, who stood waving in the middle of the dance floor.

A gasp went up from the crowd, followed by thunderous applause. People cheered and whistled. Photographers appeared from out of nowhere and began snapping so many pictures it looked like a lightning storm was striking inside the cafeteria.

This went on for several minutes, and Justin took the opportunity to search the crowd for his twin. He found him, making his way through the cheering throng towards where Debi was standing with her parents.

Justin really wanted to whisper something encouraging to Daniel, but he had his doubts about the words reaching his twin's ears through all the noise and commotion. Even wolf-hearing had its limitations.

Mayor Graham hurried to join the stars in the middle of the floor. After several more flashes, she raised her arms, calling for quiet. It took a moment for the crowd to settle down. When they did, she thrust the microphone into Jackson's hand.

'How about a little speech?' she cried.

If Jackson was surprised, he didn't let it show as he took the mic. 'For now, I'd just like

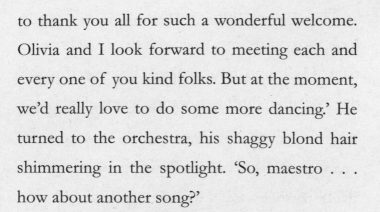

to thank you all for such a wonderful welcome. Olivia and I look forward to meeting each and every one of you kind folks. But at the moment, we'd really love to do some more dancing.' He turned to the orchestra, his shaggy blond hair shimmering in the spotlight. 'So, maestro . . . how about another song?'

The orchestra launched into a high-energy tune and a roar went up from the crowd as people flew to the dance floor.

Justin panicked. He and Riley had only practised ballroom dancing. Free-form dancing was something he'd never even thought about.

But before he could offer to lead Riley off the floor, she began to dance . . . and boy, did that girl have style!

'Where did you learn this?' Justin asked, laughing.

'I didn't learn it anywhere,' she said, her eyes

shining with confidence. 'I'm improvising! Try to keep up!'

As they 'rocked out' Justin was surprised to see Coach Johnston on the dance floor. He didn't have any natural rhythm but he was certainly giving it his all. And the best part was that his dance partner was . . . Miss Samantha!

Justin pointed this out to Riley, who laughed.

'I told you they'd hit it off!' she said.

When the song ended, Justin gave Riley a huge hug. But once again, Louis Gutterson was calling for the crowd's attention. 'It's time to announce the competitors for the dance contest.'

Justin looked at Samantha, who was clearly holding her breath. On the opposite side of the dance floor, Miranda looked positively relaxed.

'The finalists are as follows,' Gutterson drawled into the mic. 'Couples number three, number eight, number sixteen and number twenty-seven.'

As the lucky couples came forward, Justin realised that all four pairs – all eight dancers – were members of Samantha's class!

Riley let out a squeal of absolute glee. They hurried over to where Samantha was standing beside Coach Johnston.

'Congratulations,' Riley cried, hugging their teacher.

Just then, Justin felt an icy presence come up behind him. He turned to see Miranda glowering at Samantha.

'Miranda,' said Samantha, 'I thought your dancers were all quite accomplished. You should be very proud.' She gave her rival a sweet, genuine smile.

Miranda just scowled.

'Since it looks as if we'll continue to teach

across the street from one another,' Samantha went on, 'maybe we can put the past behind us and try being friends?'

Miranda's eyes narrowed, her voice a snake-like hiss: 'I don't think so.'

With that, she stalked out of the cafeteria.

Samantha sighed.

Coach Johnston smiled. Justin didn't even know the guy knew *how* to smile! 'Some people just don't understand sportsmanship,' said Coach, patting the dance teacher gently on the arm.

As Coach and Miss Samantha headed off to get some punch, Justin heard a voice that sent a cold chill down his spine.

'Yo, Packer!'

It was Kyle. The Beasts were with him.

Oh, man. Here it comes . . .

'Hey, Kyle,' Justin gulped. 'What's that?' He pointed to a piece of paper in Kyle's hand.

212

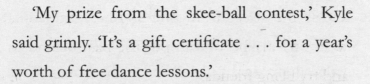

'My prize from the skee-ball contest,' Kyle said grimly. 'It's a gift certificate . . . for a year's worth of free dance lessons.'

Riley actually let out a huge snort of laugher.

Justin blinked. 'You're kidding.'

'Nope.' Kyle shook his head. 'Chris's little sister already offered to buy it off me. I told her I wanted to see if I could trade it in to the community centre for free Dog Obedience classes first. I was thinking of taking Yancy. That guy needs to work on his manners.'

Justin actually laughed, but he was still bracing himself for the worst.

'So, about that little foxtrot you just did . . .' Kyle began.

'Actually,' Justin muttered, 'it was a waltz.'

'Whatever it was . . .'

Wait for it.

'. . . It took guts.'

213

Again, Justin blinked. 'Huh?'

'It took real courage to get out there on that dance floor,' said Caleb. 'And to be honest, you kinda didn't suck.'

'Well, uh . . .' Justin shrugged, grinning. 'Thanks, guys.'

'You were great, too, Riley,' Kyle said, giving her a thumbs up. 'Way coordinated. If you were a guy, we might recruit you for Offense.'

'Thanks, Kyle.' She gave him a little punch to the arm and laughed. 'Coming from the world skee-ball champion, that means a lot.'

Riley turned to Justin with a look of glee in her eyes. 'I didn't make a fool of myself!' she said. 'More importantly, I didn't make a fool of *you*.'

'I'll always be a fool for you,' he said, wiggling his eyebrows.

'One thousand cheese points for that!' said Riley. But she was smiling, so he reckoned she

214

liked it. 'Come on, let's dance,' she said.

That was fine with Justin. He took her hand and pulled her to the centre of the floor. It was another fast number, and Justin felt as if he were on top of the world, dancing with his incredible girlfriend. Now that he knew the Beasts weren't going to mock him forever for taking dance lessons, Justin was able to enjoy himself. Everywhere he looked, people were letting loose, having a great time.

But because he was the only one lucky enough to be dancing with Riley – cheesy or not – Justin knew *he* was having the best time of all.

Chapter Eleven

After the epic fail of *not* meeting Winifred Peters, Daniel had gloomily put the unsigned copy of *Everlasting Night* in his coat pocket. Now he was standing awkwardly beside his girlfriend on the edge of the dance floor, listening to the mayor introduce the special guests.

The lack of birthday gift hung between them like an off-key note. When he'd first joined Debi, she'd smiled, but there was a lot of uncertainty behind it. Neither one had spoken since Daniel arrived.

On the upside, all that kumquat juice he'd guzzled at home seemed to be working. He was standing close to her – on her left side – and her bracelet wasn't bothering him at all.

Say something sweet, or clever, or intelligent . . . or at least say something out loud!

'You look really nice.'

'Thanks, Daniel. So do you.'

'Are you having fun?'

'I am,' she said. 'I can't believe I'm breathing the same air as Winifred Peters! And it was cool that Jackson and Olivia showed up.'

'Yeah, about Winifred Peters . . .' Daniel summoned up his courage. 'Debi, I want to explain . . .'

His hand went to the pocket of his pants, where the seashell necklace waited to be revealed. He'd brought it along, thinking they'd all get a big laugh out of it *after* he personally introduced her to her favourite author and presented the book to be signed. Now his only option was to give her the cruddy little necklace, tell her the truth, and apologise. And he was just about to.

But Mackenzie Barton showed up and, as usual, ruined everything.

'Debi!' she cried, her voice filled with mock-excitement. 'You must be so happy to see your best bud, Olivia. Why don't you go say hi?' Her eyes flashed, challenging Debi to make a move.

Daniel felt a rumbling growl in his chest.

'I'll say hi,' Debi said, unruffled. 'But I'm not about to go interrupt a couple when they're dancing.' She smiled sweetly. 'That would be unfriendly.'

Mackenzie looked ready to explode. 'What would you call *lying* about being best pals with a movie star, hmmm? I'd say that's the epiphany of unfriendly right there!'

Daniel snorted. 'The word you're looking for is "*epitome*". It was in the vocabulary test.'

But Debi remained calm. 'Oh, I never said that Olivia and I were *best* friends, I only said we –'

'Debi Morgan?' came an excited voice. 'OMG!'

Daniel watched as a pretty girl with long brown hair practically sprang off the dance floor to wrap Debi in a huge hug.

'Hi, Olivia!' said Debi. 'It's great to see you.'

'Great to see you, too!' Olivia stepped back and took both of Debi's hands in hers, beaming. 'I was just saying to Jackson the other day that I wanted to look you up the minute we got to Pine Wood. And here you are!'

Mackenzie looked ready to sprout fur and wolfify.

'Franklin Grove really misses you,' Olivia told Debi. 'But how do you like Pine Wood?'

'I love it!' said Debi. 'I do miss everyone back home, though.'

'Please tell me you're still cheering!' cried Olivia.

Debi nodded, then indicated Mackenzie. 'In fact, this is Mackenzie. She's on the squad, too.'

Olivia gave Mackenzie a polite smile. 'Nice to meet you.'

But Mackenzie, who had obviously never been addressed by a movie star before, just stood there with her mouth flapping open and closed.

'Mackenzie is the *head* cheerleader,' Debi said pointedly.

'Ahh,' said Olivia with a knowing grin. 'Are head cheerleaders here anything like the ones back home?'

'Oh, *yes*.' Debi sighed. 'It's positively uncanny.'

The two girls smiled at each other in a way that Daniel couldn't work out. Mackenzie continued to gawk, frozen to the spot.

'By the way,' said Debi, blushing just a little, 'this is my . . . this is Daniel.'

When Olivia finally got a look at Daniel she did a double-take. 'Wait . . . I could swear I was just dancing right next to you.'

Daniel grinned. 'That would be Justin, my identical twin.'

Olivia's eyes lit up. 'I'm a twin, too! Isn't it the best?'

'No complaints so far,' said Daniel. *None that I could tell you about anyway.*

'How is Ivy?' Debi asked. 'Is she back from Transylvania?'

'Oh, yes,' said Olivia, putting a hand to her chest, looking relieved. 'She's back – she decided that fancy school wasn't for her.'

Daniel frowned. 'Transylvania's a real place?'

'Yeah,' said Debi. 'But there aren't any vampires, though!'

As Debi laughed at her joke, Olivia cleared her throat and turned quickly to Daniel. 'So, do you and your brother ever switch places?' she asked, her eyebrows waggling mischievously.

'C'mon! What kind of twins would we be if we didn't?' said Daniel.

What happened next had Daniel thinking it was probably a very good thing that Mackenzie had temporarily slipped into a non-functioning state:

Jackson Caulfield came over to join them.

'Hey . . . Debi, right?' said the superstar.

'Hi, Jackson,' said Debi, calm as anything. 'Welcome to Pine Wood.'

'Happy to be here.'

Debi put her hand on Daniel's arm. 'This is my boyfriend, Daniel.'

In the next second, Mackenzie regained the power of speech and her words came out in one long, screechy breath: 'HI I'M MACKENZIE BARTON AND I THINK YOU ARE ABSOLUTELY THE MOST GORGEOUS BOY IN THE WHOLE ENTIRE WORLD AND I WOULD LOVE TO HAVE A PART IN YOUR MOVIE ESPECIALLY IF WE GET TO KISS!'

Daniel, Debi, Olivia and Jackson stared at her.

She was ogling Jackson with wide, dreamy eyes, and bouncing up and down on the balls of her feet.

'I LOVE YOU, JACKSON CAULFIELD, AND I WOULD DO ANYTHING TO MAKE YOU MINE BUT IF THAT CAN'T HAPPEN I WOULD STILL REALLY LIKE TO BE IN THE MOVIE AND DID I MENTION IT WOULD BE GREAT IF WE COULD HAVE AN ON-SCREEN KISS?'

She was talking so loudly that people around

them turned to gape. To everyone's shock – especially Jackson's – Mackenzie suddenly launched herself towards him, leaping into his arms, reminding Daniel of a crazed spider monkey.

He snuck a glance at Olivia, who looked remarkably calm. He figured this wasn't the first time she'd ever seen a girl literally throw herself at Jackson.

Jackson carefully peeled Mackenzie off his chest and set her back down.

'I'm sorry,' he said politely, 'but my movie already has a leading lady, who happens to be the only girl I ever kiss . . . on screen or off.' He grinned. 'It's in my contract.'

Daniel had never seen Mackenzie so embarrassed. Her whole face blew up red and she clenched her fists. 'No. Of course. Contract. I see . . .' She backed away, turned and then ran.

Debi seemed embarrassed. 'Jackson, Olivia, please don't base your opinion of Pine Wood on Mackenzie.'

'Yeah,' said Daniel with a wry grin. 'We're big fans, and everything, but not *that* big.' Then a thought struck him. Perhaps he could save the day after all. 'Hey, have you two gotten to know Count Vira-slash-Winifred-Peters at all?'

'Sure,' said Olivia. 'As well as anyone *could* get to know her, that is. She really keeps to herself.'

Daniel flicked his gaze over to where Winifred was sitting on the judges' platform; to his discomfort, she was staring right at him with an unreadable look on her face.

Maybe she recognises me from outside. I hope she isn't planning to call security.

But the novelist surprised Daniel by giving him a tiny grin and raising her water bottle in a toast.

A toast to what?

'Winifred sat in on the early table reads of the script,' Jackson explained. 'She was really nice, but super shy and reserved. And now that that phase of production is over, we have to go through her agent if we want to talk to her.'

Daniel felt himself crumbling. 'So I don't suppose you'd be able to arrange an introduction tonight?'

'Doubtful, man. Sorry.' Jackson looked genuinely apologetic.

'It's OK,' sighed Daniel. 'I should have known it wouldn't work. When I tried to meet her earlier tonight, it was pretty obvious she wasn't interested in making new acquaintances.'

'What?' Debi whirled to give Daniel a quizzical look. 'Daniel, why would you want to meet Winifred Peters?'

At that moment, Jackson's cellphone rang. He

checked the screen, then gave them a sheepish look. 'I hate to sound like a self-important Hollywood big-shot here, but this is my agent.'

'We should really take the call,' said Olivia. 'Debi, let's meet over at the punch bowl in five minutes. I want to catch up!'

When the movie stars were gone, Debi turned back to Daniel. 'Daniel, tell me . . . *why* were you trying to talk to Winifred?'

Time to come clean. 'I had a plan. But it failed. I wanted to arrange a personal introduction for you. As part of your birthday present.'

Debi's eyes shone. 'Daniel, that's the sweetest thing I've ever heard.'

'Wait,' he said glumly. 'It gets sweeter. I had Riley swipe your copy of *Everlasting Night* and I was going to have Count Winifred Vira Peters autograph it for you.'

'Oh, Daniel!' Debi looked like she might

melt. 'Best gift idea *ever*!'

'That's the problem. It's still just an *idea*. I couldn't upgrade it to actual *reality*.'

'Well, just knowing that I have a boyfriend determined to get me something wonderful makes up for everything.'

Daniel gave her a half-smile. 'Even this?' He reached into his pocket and withdrew the seashell necklace. 'It's your original present. I had it with me at Chez Fraud . . .'

'Chez *Claude*.'

'Right. But I didn't want to give it to you after Riley gave you that great book and your parents gave you that silver bracelet.'

Debi tore off the paper and opened the box. 'Seashells!' she cried, delighted. 'I love it.'

'You do?'

She nodded. 'Here, help me put it on.' She arranged the string of tiny shells around her neck, then held it in place as she turned around for Daniel to fasten it.

But as he reached for the clasp, his fingers brushed hers; a terrible itching began in his nose!

Oh, no. The kumquat juice must be wearing off!

Somehow, he managed to stifle the sneeze and get the necklace fastened. When she lowered her hands, it improved things slightly, but he knew he'd be in trouble if he didn't find some of that nasty-tasting drink – and fast!

'You should go talk to Olivia,' he said, 'so you can have some time to talk in private before she gets swamped by fans.'

'OK,' said Debi. 'Wait right here, because when I'm done catching up with Olivia, I'm going to come back and ask my boyfriend to dance with me.'

Daniel managed a grin. 'I'm pretty sure he'll accept.'

With that, she headed across the room, leaving Daniel to panic over where he might get his hands on the antidote. He was pretty sure the punch was kumquat-free. There was no way he could dance with Debi now. If he wasn't the biggest let-down in a boyfriend ever, then –

'Hello, Daniel!'

Daniel spun to see Mr Morgan standing behind him.

'H-hello, Mr Morgan,' Daniel stammered. 'Debi just went over to –'

'I'm looking for you,' Debi's dad said coolly. 'I have a very important question to ask you.' Daniel's stomach swirled like the merry-go-round ride at the amusement park. 'You remember the silver bracelet Debi's mother and I gave her for her birthday?'

'Yes, sir.' *I only wish I could forget it!*

'Well, I thought maybe you could tell me if

you think she'd like *this*.'

Mr Morgan removed a long, slender box from the breast pocket of his sport coat and held it out towards Daniel.

'What is it?'

'It's the gift her mother and I are planning to give her for Christmas. I brought it along tonight to get your opinion,' Mr Morgan explained, an eyebrow raised. 'After all, you *are* her boyfriend, and I figure a *normal* boy would be able to tell if his girlfriend would like a particular gift.'

There was something about the way he had stressed the word *normal* . . .

'Have a look, will you?' Mr Morgan opened the box with a knowing grin.

Inside was a heavy silver chain. A necklace to match the bracelet, only much longer and thicker. And much more silver.

Silver Doom's big brother!

Daniel's eyes stung and his nose felt as though it had caught fire. The lingering effects of his kumquat binge kept him from outright sneezing but his discomfort must have been written all over his face.

This was a test! Mr Morgan *did* suspect Daniel's Lupine secret. Daniel turned away from the necklace fast and lowered his head. 'It's nice,' he choked out, desperately trying to hold back a sneeze.

'Something wrong, son?' Mr Morgan prodded. 'Don't you like silver?'

'Well, um . . .'

'Oh! Isn't that lovely!'

At the sound of a woman's voice, Daniel looked up. Winifred Peters – *the* Winifred Peters – was now standing beside Mr Morgan, smiling down at the jewellery box.

'Count Vira!' A huge smile spread across Mr

Morgan's face. 'I mean, Ms Peters! It's . . . It's . . . It's an honour.'

Perhaps distracted by the arrival of the famous – not to mention his own personal favourite – author, Debi's dad seemed to forget all about the chain and Daniel's weird reaction to it.

'I answer to both,' Winifred Peters said with a chuckle, 'but you may call me Winnie.' She extended her hand to shake.

A flustered Mr Morgan immediately tucked the box back into his pocket so he could accept the writer's handshake. Daniel took a deep, grateful breath of silver-free air.

'It's an honour to meet you, ma'am,' said Mr Morgan. 'I'm a big fan.'

'Thank you,' she said.

Then she did the strangest thing. As Winifred continued to shake Mr Morgan's hand, she casually reached into her purse and pulled out

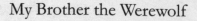

a fresh water bottle, then slipped it to Daniel behind her back.

It only took him a second to realise what was happening.

She was rescuing him! The bottle she'd been sipping from all night didn't contain mere water . . . it contained kumquat juice.

Winifred Peters is a werewolf! Maybe she-wolves aren't as 'rare' as my dad thinks!

Daniel opened the bottle and drank half of it in one gulp. 'Now,' said Winifred, 'about that gorgeous necklace. Is it a gift for someone special?'

'It's a Christmas present for my daughter, Debi.'

'How nice,' said Winifred, sipping from her own bottle.

'Since I'm her boyfriend,' Daniel said, 'Mr Morgan was asking me for my opinion.' He turned a big, confident grin to Debi's dad. 'May I see the necklace again, sir?'

Mr Morgan looked confused. 'You *want* to see it?'

'Well, how else can I tell you what I think?'

Mr Morgan frowned, but took the box from his pocket. This time Daniel reached right in and removed the necklace. He even held it up to his face to examine it closely. 'I think she'll definitely dig it,' he declared. 'Silver totally rocks.' He put the necklace around his wrist to make the point. 'Maybe I will get her something similar next year. Matching earrings, maybe.'

Mr Morgan's scowl lightened, and then he started to smile.

'May I?' asked Winifred.

'Sure.' Daniel handed her the necklace, and as she cooed over the 'exquisite quality' of the 'delicate links', he had to clamp his mouth shut to keep from cracking up. No way could Mr Morgan suspect either of them of being wolves now.

When Winifred gave the necklace back to Mr Morgan, Daniel said, 'Ms Peters, the reason I was trying to get your attention outside earlier was because my girlfriend is actually a huge fan of yours.'

'That's nice to hear,' she said.

'Her birthday was a little while ago. I was hoping that you'd let me introduce you to her, and sign her copy of *Everlasting Night*. If I could make that happen, it would be the best gift ever.'

'It would be my pleasure to assist you in making such a heartfelt gesture,' Winifred said, smiling primly. She turned to Mr Morgan. 'Where is your daughter?'

'I'll get her,' said Mr Morgan, then he took off at a trot, eager to find Debi.

'I can't believe it!' whispered Daniel. 'You're a she-wolf.'

'Talk about a plot twist, hmm?' she said.

'But how did you know *I* was a werewolf?'

'Writers tend to be more intuitive than most. I saw something in your eyes when you approached me earlier and I just knew we were alike.'

'So why did you run away?'

Winifred looked a little guilty. 'I was afraid you were going to ask me to settle here among your community.'

Daniel felt a twinge of hurt. 'Would that be so bad?'

'I suppose not. But I like my solitude.'

'Well, thanks for bailing me out with that kumquat juice,' Daniel said.

'My pleasure. You see, I learned a long time ago to always keep some close at hand.' Now Winifred's face turned serious. 'I was wondering if you might do me a favour.'

'Sure! Name it!'

'Well, there's a young she-wolf here tonight...'

'Emma,' Daniel gasped. 'You know her?'

'No. Like with you, I knew her when I saw her. I was hoping you'd look after her; be a friend.'

'We are already friends,' Daniel assured her. 'And I'd be happy to look after Emma. She's a great person.'

'Thank you, Daniel,' said Winifred. 'She reminds me so much of myself at that age.'

'Speaking of being that age, can I ask you a question . . . when Emma first showed up in Pine Wood, a weird thing happened. All the other guys who are . . . ya know, wolfish . . . they started showing off like crazy whenever Emma was around.'

'Yes.' Winifred gave a frustrated huff. 'It can get rather tedious.'

Daniel grinned. 'What I don't understand is why it never happened to *me*. I never once felt the need to try to impress Emma at all. I thought it had something to do with my nose being stuffed because of Debi's silver bracelet.'

Winifred nodded. 'That was definitely a factor,' she said. Then she smiled that wistful smile again. 'But maybe there was a bigger reason.'

'Like what?' *Is there something wrong with me after all? Am I a weirdo werewolf, as well as a weirdo human?*

'It could be Debi herself.'

'Huh?'

'When a young cub falls in love . . . he won't notice other girls – Lupine or human – because he's taken, heart and soul.'

'Wow,' said Daniel.

Could that be true? Could he be in love with Debi? No way – he was too young, too cool to . . . but he didn't have long to think about it because Debi and her father came rushing over. His heart flip-flopped and he wondered if Winifred might be on to something.

239

Debi was positively giddy as she grabbed Winifred's hand and shook it.

Daniel smiled, feeling a burst of pride at how happy his 'gift' was making his girlfriend. He took the book out of his jacket pocket and handed it to Winifred.

'Would you mind signing this for Debi please?' he asked.

'A pleasure!' she said, and she signed it in beautiful penmanship:

To Debi. Always believe in the moonlight, for that is where true love awaits. Best wishes, Winifred Peters.

("Count Vira")

Then Winifred excused herself to go consult with the other dance judges before the contest began. When she was gone, Mr Morgan gave Daniel a pat on the back.

'That was a great present, son,' he said gruffly. 'You've got good taste.'

'Back at you, sir,' said Daniel, nodding towards Mr Morgan's pocket.

'What did *that* mean?' Debi asked, as her father walked away.

'Never mind,' said Daniel. 'Now, I seem to remember something about you asking your boyfriend to dance.'

Debi took his hand and led him on to the floor. Daniel put his arms around her waist, and she placed her hands on his shoulders. Silver Doom was mere inches from his face, but he didn't so much as sniffle.

Gotta hand it to those she-wolves, he thought. *They sure know how to help a cub out.*

As they danced, Daniel took a moment to look around at the other couples on the floor. He smiled at Emma – who was dancing with Otto!

– and he waved to Justin and Riley, who were dancing beside Jackson and Olivia.

Emto, Jiley and Jando? He laughed, realising that it really didn't matter what anyone called them . . . the important thing was that they were happy.

Probably not as happy as him, but still.

'And another thing,' said Debi in a thoughtful tone. 'I love what Winifred Peters wrote in my book, but what do you think she meant? About the moonlight?'

Daniel shrugged. 'That moonlight is romantic?'

Debi frowned. 'I just have this feeling there was more to it than that. Like it was a message.'

Daniel shrugged, smiled and pulled her closer.

But of course, Debi was absolutely right. There was a very special message hidden in that inscription and he knew exactly what it was: Winifred was referring to how, for centuries, werewolves the world over had come to find their true selves in the moon's glimmering light.

And because Daniel was one of those wolves, the inscription was clearly Winifred's way of telling Debi that wherever Daniel was, that's where Debi would find her true love.

As they moved to the music, Daniel wished he could explain the message properly. But he knew in his heart this wasn't the right time.

Someday, he thought, *she will know everything about me.*

That would be amazing.But for now, all he wanted was to just enjoy the moment.

He had Debi in his arms. And that was enough.

Pine Wood Post
Online Feature

Repartee With Riley

Or, should this be 'Exchanges With Emma'? This week, I get to take a well-earned break (and, believe me, it is!) and am handing over to Pine Wood Junior High's newest addition, Emma Sharpe — who is here to introduce herself so that everyone can get to know her. Be nice in the comments — that means you, Kyle, Caleb and co . . . (Although I doubt that will be a problem this time! *ahem*)

Hello, everyone!

Thanks to Riley for letting me muscle in on her weekly article. I'll do my best to live up to her standard of humour and energy . . . Although anyone who has seen Riley at work will know how hard it is to keep up with her. (Even *me* . . .)

So, where to begin? Well I'm just so thrilled that Pine Wood turned out to be a cool town, with even cooler people. Honestly, I was worried that I might not fit in. I know lots of people our age tend to feel like this but, for me, this has been a real hurdle to jump.

Thankfully I've got better at jumping in the last year or so (a *lot* better), but it is just so great to be at a school where the hurdles have been put where they belong . . . on the school track, and not in the hallways and cafeteria.

Not that there are many people at our school who would have trouble jumping hurdles! In fact, I think there's one or two – or *ten* – 9th graders who could entertain themselves for hours jumping, cartwheeling and somersaulting back and forth over any hurdle that was put in front of them!

I know that there are probably a few boys out there blushing right now, but seriously – I was so charmed by everyone's efforts to welcome me to the new school. It made everything a *lot* less frightening, so thank you all.

One of the best parts about starting a new school is getting to meet new people, and I've not met *nearly* enough of you! I hope to fix this in the coming days and weeks. So that we have something to talk about, I can tell you the following things about me:

1.   I like most arts- and craftsy-type things, although lately I have come to the DEPRESSING conclusion that I just don't have delicate enough claws to sew and knit as well as I would like to. Did I say 'claws'? I meant HANDS!

2.   Embarrassing confession – I'm kind of scared of the dark, and spooky places. You won't catch me anywhere near Lycan Point, for example! Nope. Nuh-huh. NEVER.

3.   My favourite type of music is loud, loud, LOUD. The louder the drum solo, the better!

There! That should be enough for you to get started. I'm really looking forward to making lots of friends in Pine Wood.

COMMENTS ON THIS FEATURE:

MACKENZIE BARTON says: There are actually ELEVEN members in a football offensive squad, not ten. I do hope you're not thinking of trying out to be a cheerleader.

CALEB DEVLIN says: Mackenzie, you apologize right now!

EGMONT PRESS: ETHICAL PUBLISHING

Egmont Press is about turning writers into successful authors and children into passionate readers – producing books that enrich and entertain. As a responsible children's publisher, we go even further, considering the world in which our consumers are growing up.

Safety First
Naturally, all of our books meet legal safety requirements. But we go further than this; every book with play value is tested to the highest standards – if it fails, it's back to the drawing-board.

Made Fairly
We are working to ensure that the workers involved in our supply chain – the people that make our books – are treated with fairness and respect.

Responsible Forestry
We are committed to ensuring all our papers come from environmentally and socially responsible forest sources.

**For more information, please visit our website at
www.egmont.co.uk/ethical**